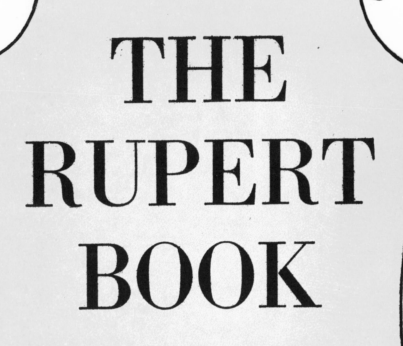

THE
RUPERT
BOOK

DAILY EXPRESS
PUBLICATIONS

Printed in Great Britain by
Greycaine Limited, Watford, Herts.
1941

Original edition published 1941
This facsimile edition printed in Italy
and published under licence by Pedigree Books Limited
©1993 Express Newspapers PLC, London

CONTENTS

RUPERT and the
RED EGG

When Rupert be-
gan collecting
stamps he started
on a dangerous
adventure --but he
got his stamps

RUPERT STARTS COLLECTING

"Oh Rupert," Willie cries, "do look!
My Daddy's buying me this book;

"We're stamp collecting, so would you
Come in and join our stamp club, too?"

So Rupert to his father flies:
"An album give me, please," he cries.

Says Mr. Bear, "Well, I'll agree
When fifty stamps you show to me."

"I wonder what Rex and Willie Whiskers are so interested in," thinks Rupert, as he notices two of his pals gazing intently into a bookshop. Being very inquisitive, he joins them. "Look, Rupert," cries Willie, "some of us have begun stamp-collecting. We're starting a stamp club, and my daddy's giving me an album just like that one. Won't you join the club, too?" "Rather! I'd love to," says the little bear.

Delighted with the new idea, he runs home to ask his father about it. "Please, may I have a stamp album?" he begs. Mr. Bear smiles to see Rupert's enthusiasm. Then he looks wise and says quietly: "You're beginning at the wrong end, Rupert. How do I know you'll keep it up? You'd better begin collecting first. When you have fifty different stamps you can come to me again and we'll think about that album."

Rupert and the Red Egg

RUPERT ASKS THE POSTMAN

The postman's coming down the street,
And Rupert runs his friend to greet;

He hopes in stamps to do a deal;
"Why," laughs the postman, "I can't steal."

A parcel bearing foreign stamps
He carries as he onward tramps.

"I'll beg those stamps," thinks Rupert Bear;
"The owner may be kind and share."

Rupert is a little disappointed, but he can see that his father is right. Rounding a corner he sees the village postman. "Why, of course, he's the very man to ask," thinks the little bear, trotting up to him. But the postman only roars with laughter. "Ho, ho," he chuckles, "you do get some ideas, Rupert. It's more than my job's worth to start taking stamps off people's letters."

The postman heaves a heavy parcel that he is delivering over his shoulder and makes off across the common. The little bear notices that there are two very interesting looking stamps on the parcel. "If I could find out where that parcel goes perhaps I could ask the people to give me the stamps," he mutters. He catches the postman again and watches carefully where he goes.

9

RUPERT MEETS PONG PING

He's glad to see the postman bring
The parcel to his friend, Pong-Ping.

"Those stamps, Pong-Ping, do give me please;"
"All right," says Pong-Ping, "they're Chinese."

"I get a present every year
From Uncle; stay and see what's here."

Now when the parcel is outspread
It's full of eggs—and one is red.

After watching the postman for some time Rupert sees with excitement that he delivers the parcel at the house of his pal Pong-Ping, the Peke. The little Peke is astonished to see Rupert and to hear his request. "Yes, you can have the stamps. They're Chinese," he says, "I've got some more just like them."

Rupert has got his stamps and is turning to go when Pong-Ping calls him back. "Wouldn't you like to come in and see what's in my parcel?" he asks. "My uncle in China sends me a box like this every year. They're Chinese eggs," explains Pong-Ping, "and they're topping to eat." "My, aren't they whoppers!" cries Rupert. "And, look, one of them is red. What is the red egg?" Pong-Ping is puzzled. "I don't know," he confesses; "I've never had a red egg before."

RUPERT GETS AN EGG

Says courtly Pong-Ping, "Take this egg,
And tell me how it tastes, I beg."

Then Rupert the Professor meets,
"Why, Rupert, what's that egg?" he greets.

He looks at it with great surprise;
"Whatever bird laid this?" he cries.

And then, when Rupert turns to go,
He shouts, "Don't eat it till you know."

At length Rupert says it is time for him to go home. "Well," says Pong-Ping, "there are more eggs here than I shall ever eat. You take this one home with you." On his way home the little bear meets his friend, the old Professor, out for a walk. To his surprise the old man stops and looks quite excited when he catches sight of the egg.

The old Professor seems so interested that Rupert lets him handle the red egg. "I've never seen anything a bit like it," says the old man. "I'd give a lot to know what bird laid it. Are you going to have it hatched out?" "Why, no," says Rupert. "It's Chinese, and Pong-Ping says it's very good to eat. I'm taking it to my mother." Saying good-bye, he goes on his way. The Professor scratches his head. in perplexity. "I wouldn't risk eating that thing."

RUPERT RETURNS THE EGG

"An egg so big," says Mrs. Bear,
"We'll scramble, then we all can share."

But when she strikes it with a whack
Upon her basin, it won't crack.

Perhaps if boiled it still won't break,
So to Pong-Ping the egg he'll take.

And he's amazed when birds fly round
To ask, "What IS that egg you've found?"

Reaching his home Rupert shows his mother the strange red egg. "Pong-Ping wants us to eat it and tell him what it tastes like," he says. "Dear me," says Mrs. Bear doubtfully; "it looks very queer. And, besides, it's so big. It would feed the whole family. Well, let's try it scrambled and see what it looks like." Getting a basin she taps the egg on the edge, but the shell refuses to crack. She

bangs it harder and harder without any result. Having failed to break the egg, Mrs. Bear gets a saucepan so that she can boil it; but Rupert has other ideas. "No," he says, "if we can't break the shell now we might not be able to break it even when it is boiled. I'm going back to ask what Pong-Ping thinks about it." On his way he is followed by some inquisitive birds. "Whatever is it?" they chirp.

Rupert and the Red Egg

RUPERT GETS A SHOCK

When Pong-Ping hears he says, "No doubt,
It's Uncle's joke, he's caught us out."

They lay it down, it starts to roll,
And seems to be beyond control.

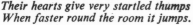

Their hearts give very startled thumps
When faster round the room it jumps.

But Rupert sees it must be trapped;
And in a cloth the egg is wrapped.

Rupert arrives breathless at Pong-Ping's house and pours out his story. "It's all very mysterious," says the little Peke; "I do believe my uncle in China is playing a practical joke on me and sent me one that is made of china!" They put it on the floor and gaze at it, feeling very puzzled. Suddenly they start. The egg has begun to roll slowly away from them.

Rupert and Pong-Ping are speechless with surprise as the egg moves by itself. Gradually it gets faster until it is giving little bounces all over the room. The two pals back away and watch its antics in frightened silence. Then Rupert pulls himself together, gets a cloth and picks up the egg still squirming. "I wish I knew what it was going to do," quavers Pong-Ping. "I'm scared of it."

Rupert and the Red Egg

RUPERT MEETS THE DWARF

He says, "My old Professor friend
His help to us will kindly lend."

So to the old man's house he flies
And there, outside, the dwarf he spies.

The dwarf gives quite a frightened shout
To see an egg that jumps about;

And when it tumbles on the ground
The birds, astonished, flutter round.

For a long time Rupert and Pong-Ping stand undecided what to do, and the red egg keeps jumping about inside the cloth. Then the little bear makes up his mind. "I'm going to see the old Professor," he declares; "he saw the egg when I first had it and he warned me against it. This will interest him, even if he can't explain it." Off he runs, right over the hill until the Professor's queer house comes in view.

The dwarf is very startled when Rupert shows him what he has in the cloth. The red egg is now so active that the little bear can hardly hold it. At length it falls and rolls round a tree. At once it is surrounded by inquisitive birds, who fly round and peck at it viciously, but they make no impression on the hard shell. "There's something very odd about this thing," says an old crow.

RUPERT ASKS THE PROFESSOR

*One says, "The King of Birds must hear
Where he can find that egg, my dear."*

*Says Rupert, "To the master wise
I'm going," then away he flies.*

*The master to his bookshelf turns:
"Eggs—red," he looks for; nothing learns.*

*He sees the stamps, but in his books
In vain through "Eggs—Chinese," he looks.*

When Rupert picks the egg up again a beautiful bird flies to him and cries: "Do tell me where you are taking that red egg. I'm off to tell the King of the Birds all about it, and he is sure to want to know where to find it." "I'm going down the hill to the old Professor's house. He may be able to tell us something," replies Rupert. And, entering the grounds, he finds his old friend pottering in the garden.

The old Professor gets very excited at the development of the red egg and hurries to his library to see if he can find any mention of such an egg or of a bird which lays it. Rupert suddenly thinks of the two stamps from Pong-Ping's parcel and he produces them from his pocket. "Ah, that's a help," says the old man; "those stamps show what part of China the egg came from."

RUPERT GETS A RIDE

The dwarf says, looking rather queer,
"A strange new visitor is here.

"On Rupert he has come to call,
You'll find him up this staircase tall."

It is a bird who here has sped;
His king would see the egg so red.

He picks up Rupert in his claws,
And through the sky he swiftly soars.

At length the old Professor gives a sigh. "The problem has beaten me," he says. All at once they are interrupted by the little dwarf who opens the door and looks rather scared. "There's an extraordinary visitor who says he wants to see Rupert," quavers the dwarf. To Rupert's surprise he doesn't go to the main door but leads them to a spiral staircase that seems to go to the roof.

Sure enough the dwarf leads Rupert and the old Professor out on to the roof, where they are startled to see an enormous bird with a badge round its neck. The bird smiles and bows to Rupert. "I come from the King of Birds," says the great creature. "His Majesty has heard of a wonderful red egg which you possess, and he requests that you let him see it." The bird seizes him suddenly in its talons.

RUPERT SHOWS THE EGG

They cross some mountains gleaming bright,
And reach at length a palace white.

There crowds of flying songsters bring
Bewildered Rupert to their King.

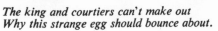

The king and courtiers can't make out
Why this strange egg should bounce about.

The king says, "Tell the giant hen,
To hatch it, and we'll all know then."

The great bird makes wonderful speed and rises higher and higher. At first Rupert is very frightened, but the grip of the talons is so firm that he soon loses his fear and looks down at the curious country that is far below. They glide down, surrounded by hundreds of other birds, until Rupert finds himself landed safely on a terrace and facing the King of the Birds in his gorgeous clothes.

The King of the Birds shows great interest in the red egg and soon his attendants and the important birds of his Court are standing around and gazing at it with astonishment as it rolls and bounces about the terrace. "Never have I seen an egg do that," declares the King. "If it really is an egg it may be possible to hatch it. Go and command the giant hen to do her best with it."

RUPERT SEES THE DRAGON

The giant hen is most distressed;
That jumping egg gives her no rest.

But Rupert quite enjoys the joke,
Until she squawks and he sees smoke.

Away the hen in panic flies,
And Rupert, in the nest, espies

A dragon fierce, with glittering scales,
Who clouds of scorching smoke exhales.

The giant hen is very surprised at the job she has been given, but she cannot disobey the King's orders, so the egg is put in a lot of straw and she sits on it to keep it warm. "It may be a long time hatching," says the Court official. "We'd better go back to the King." They set off but have only gone a few yards when there is a loud cry from behind them, and, turning, Rupert sees a wisp of smoke from the place they have just left.

Hurrying back Rupert finds that clouds of smoke are coming from the place he has left. He arrives just in time to see the giant hen give a terrified squawk and fly off her nest, leaving fragments of the red egg in the straw, and in the middle of them is an extraordinary little creature with glittering scales, and breathing smoke and looking very fierce. "Good gracious!" gasps the little bear, "it isn't a bird at all!"

RUPERT SENDS FOR PONG PING

The birds are quickly on the wing
As Rupert runs the alarm to bring.

And with the dragon close behind
He climbs a tree, escape to find.

Now there the Messenger he sees,
And so he begs, "Fetch Pong-Ping, please;

He's Chinese, so his help do get;
I'll go back to the parapet."

Rupert loses no time in warning all the birds. He rushes back to the terrace shouting at the top of his voice. "Look out! fly for your lives! The giant hen has hatched out a dragon!" The little dragon, leaping about with surprising strength, bounds towards Rupert, who takes to his heels, scrambles on to the parapet, and just manages to spring into the branches of a tree. Most of the birds are afraid to return to the terrace, and Rupert is worried. "It's my fault that the red egg came here," he thinks unhappily. Then he notices the huge King's messenger bird. "You'd better go back to Nutwood and fetch my friend Pong-Ping," he says. "He's from China, and may know how to deal with dragons." The bird seizes the idea, and when it has flown away Rupert screws up his courage and returns to the parapet.

Rupert and the Red Egg

RUPERT LISTENS TO PONG PING

His action next is quite unwise:
The dragon's attitude he tries;

But it's so fierce, he takes a spring
Back to the wall, and there's Pong-Ping.

"Well," Pong-Ping says, "you all must learn
That his hot breath your home will burn.

So first, please slake his appetite
With fruit, that will his greed delight."

Becoming bolder, he slips down from the parapet and approaches it cautiously. But the little creature is not at all friendly. It hisses ferociously, and poor Rupert, getting scared of its sharp teeth and it's hot breath, hurriedly regains his place of safety. Then he anxiously watches the sky until to his joy the huge bird reappears and makes for the palace, bearing his friend Pong-Ping in its talons.

Pong-Ping is amazed to hear Rupert's story and to see the glittering dragon that came out of the red egg. "You must get him away before he grows too big," he says, "or he'll burn your palace down with his hot breath. I'll tell you how to set about it. First, you must get him lots of food. Dragons have terrific appetites." Calling one of the Court birds to him Pong-Ping gives his instructions.

RUPERT WATCHES THE FEAST

The dragon gulps the fruit so sweet
Then strolls off, feeling quite replete.

The friends behind him softly creep
And find him in his nest asleep.

Then Pong-Ping, lifting him with pride,
Says, "In a cloth he must be tied.

"And him the messenger can take
To Dragons' Land before he'll wake."

The dragon sets to work sampling all the fruit and gobbling it up at a great rate. Gradually to their relief the queer creature takes on a more contented expression and breathes less smoke. At length he seems to have had enough and, looking a good deal stouter, he goes gently back to his box, and falls asleep. "Now he's quite harmless," says Pong-Ping; "you can pick him up if you like."

They put it in a large cloth, and the King of the Birds, who had been keeping under cover, comes out to look at the strange sight. "Now is your chance to get him away," says Pong-Ping. "He will probably sleep for about three days, so you must get your fast messenger to carry him over the mountains of China and put him down where all the other dragons live."

RUPERT SENDS THE DRAGON

The message bird, though feeling blue
When given this odious task to do,

Takes up the bundle in his claws,
And sets his course for China's shores.

The king says, "Rupert, you must stay
While my strong messenger's away."

"At home they'll worry," Rupert cries,
Then hears a whirring in the skies.

Rupert and Pong-Ping fasten the dragon up in the cloth, and the King of Birds with his Court Chamberlain go to give instructions to the great messenger. The huge bird doesn't like the idea very much and says so. "I'm being given an awful lot of work to do to-day," he grumbles, "first fetching Rupert and then Pong-Ping, and now having to fly a dragon all the way to China!"

When the great bird is out of sight Rupert turns to the King of the Birds. "That should be the end of your trouble," he says. "Please send us home now, my mummy and daddy will be worrying," cries Rupert. Suddenly he stops. A loud noise is coming from the sky. Looking up, the two pals see an extraordinary machine descending towards them from the clouds.

RUPERT TELLS THE PROFESSOR

They see a strange machine descend;
"Come on," shouts Rupert, "that's my friend."

Yes, it's the Master, and they run,
To tell him all that they have done.

Then Rupert takes him to the king,
Who kindly tells him everything.

And he and Rupert plan to take
The eggshell as a rare keepsake.

Rupert and Pong-Ping watch the queer machine as it drops lower and finally lands just outside the Palace. "I believe I know who it must be," he cries. As Rupert had hoped, the figure who comes striding towards them is none other than his friend the old Professor.

Rupert is very happy to see his friend, and quickly takes the old Professor to introduce him to the King of the Birds. "I was so inquisitive about that strange red egg," says the old man, "that I had to follow Rupert here and see what your opinion is." The King smiles and tells him all about the dragon, while the Professor listens in amazement and can hardly believe it until Rupert shows him the fragments of the egg. "Those pieces are very rare and valuable," says the old man. "I must have some for my collection."

RUPERT GETS HIS STAMPS

The king now bids them all good-bye
And soon they're roaring through the sky.

Then as the strange machine descends
His Master kind the dwarf attends.

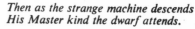

And while the Master mounts the shell
The friends the stamp club story tell.

The old man says, "Stamps?   Here's a store,
So take your choice, I've plenty more."

Rupert and Pong-Ping and the old Professor all put pieces of the precious egg in their pockets and then say good-bye to the King of the Birds.   Then Rupert and Pong-Ping squeeze into the tiny cockpit beside the old man.   Soon they are crossing great mountains and wild country, until they descend to find the dwarf waiting on the roof of the Professor's house.

Once inside the Professor's house Rupert and Pong-Ping help the old man to mount his fragments of the red egg and put them in a frame.   Then they put them into a cabinet with lots of other precious things. Before saying good-bye Rupert tells him how the adventure started, and how he wants fifty different stamps. "Why," says the old man heartily, picking up an envelope, "I've lots of stamps here.   Choose fifty of them for yourself.   They're all good ones.'

RUPERT RETURNS HOME

Then Rupert quickly homeward goes,
The stamps and eggshell red he shows.

Says Mrs. Bear, "Well, I declare!
This eggshell as a brooch I'll wear."

The album Rupert's father buys,
And Rupert to his playmates flies.

"Help fix my stamps," is his request,
They do, and vote his batch the best.

Thanking the old Professor for his gift, Rupert says good-bye to him and to Pong-Ping and scampers home to tell his parents all about his adventure. Mrs. Bear is eager to hear what happened to the strange red egg which she had been unable to break, and gasps in horror when she hears that there was a dragon in it. But she is delighted with the piece of eggshell which Rupert has brought, and she runs to a mirror. "It's a lovely colour!" she declares; "I shall have it made into a brooch."

Finally, Rupert shows his father the fifty different stamps. "My word, you've been quick," says Mr. Bear, "and you've a very original way of collecting stamps."

And, true to his promise, he goes with him to the bookshop and buys him an album.

RUPERT

and

BABY BADGER

Telling how wise
old Mr. Goat
solved the mystery
of the missing
Baby Badger

RUPERT MEETS BILL

Football the chums have planned to play,
So blow the ball up straight away,

Says Rupert, "Now we'll have a spree,
But we're one short; who can it be?"

While others play, poor Rupert sighs;
"I wish that Bill were here," he cries,

And then he runs and gives a shout,
Bill's taking Baby Brother out.

It is Saturday, and Rupert has arranged to play football with his pals. He gets his ball from the cupboard and finds that it is too soft to use. However, with the help of Pong Ping the Peke he manages to blow it up tight with a bicycle pump. Then they hurry to the common, and punctually to time they see the others running towards them. Rupert pauses. "There seems to be someone missing." The little pals are soon playing gaily. As Podgy is the fattest they make him goalkeeper between two piles of twigs. But Rupert is not quite happy. His best friend, Bill Badger, hasn't turned up. Then he notices a little figure on the horizon. "That looks like Bill," he thinks, "and I do believe he's pushing a pram! I must go and see how long he will be." Leaving the others to their game, he hurries away.

RUPERT SEES THE BABY

Soon Rupert catches up with Bill,
Who says his mother's slightly ill;

Laughs Rupert, "Fancy trusting you!
I'll come and see just what you do."

They see some berries by the way;
And think the child with them can play,

Then Rupert, gathering berries red,
Hears angry voices just ahead.

"Hi! What are you doing?" cries Rupert. "We were expecting you at football." "No football for me," sighs Bill. "My mother isn't well, so I have to take my little brother for a walk." "H'm," says Rupert doubtfully, "I'm surprised at her trusting you! I think I'd better come with you or you'll be sure to get into mischief some way or other."

"Look at those beautiful berries," cries Rupert.

"I'm sure the baby would like those to play with," and he scrambles up into the hedge while Bill pushes the pram slowly onwards.

Within a minute Rupert hears the sound of quarrelling, and one of the voices is Bill's! "Oh dear," sighs the little bear, "he's getting into mischief again. I knew he would as soon as he's left alone. I suppose I'd better go and see what he's up to."

RUPERT GETS A SHOCK

"See Bill the Nurse," the Foxes jeer;
Cries Bill, "I'll teach you lads to sneer."

He chases them with all his might;
"I must," thinks Rupert, "help him fight."

Then Rupert, running, sees with fear
The pram begin to disappear.

Upon a road that slopes downhill,
It's heading for a dangerous spill.

Coming in sight of Bill, Rupert finds that Freddy and Ferdy Fox are sitting on a fence laughing. "Yah," jeers Ferdy, "look at Bill the nursemaid!" "I'll teach you to laugh at me," shouts Bill. He rushes at them so furiously that they turn tail and run away with Bill after them. "Hi, come back," cries Rupert, as he prepares to follow. "You can't fight the pair of them." "Oh dear," he thinks.

"Bill really is an exasperating sort of pal to have! I've got to help him or he may get knocked about." Rupert dashes across the field, but, glancing over his shoulder, he gives a gasp of dismay, for the pram is not where Bill left it.

Leaving Bill to his own resources, he regains the fence, only to find that the pram is now careering towards the bridge over the river.

RUPERT FOLLOWS BABY

The baby thinks the ride is fun,
And laughs to see poor Rupert run,

He falls, the pram takes one big leap,
And bounces in the river deep.

Now Rupert from the parapet
Observes the pram is floating yet;

He makes the bank without delay.
But towering boulders block his way.

Running at his best speed, Rupert manages to gain a little on the pram. The Baby Badger thinks it is great fun and chuckles and crows in delight, but the little bear is very anxious. To make things worse, the pram leaves the path as it approaches the bridge. Rupert makes a desperate effort to grab it, but his foot strikes a stone and as he falls he sees to his horror that pram and baby have shot straight over the bank and into the water. Gaining the bridge, Rupert sees to his great relief that the pram is floating right side up. By this time the baby is struggling and crying with fright. Then the river enters a little gorge and he can no longer follow the edge. "Oh, I do hope he won't sink before I can get over the hill and reach him," thinks Rupert dismally.

RUPERT SHOWS THE WAY

Then, running round for help, he sees
Old Mr. Pug beside the trees;

"Help! Mr. Pug, help!" Rupert cries,
And then to tell his tale he tries.

"My fishing rod," says Pug, "I'll use,
To stop that pram's most dangerous cruise."

He casts his line with steady hand,
Then hooks the pram and pulls towards land.

Leaving the cliffs, Rupert runs over a little hill and without daring to stop he makes for the lower reach of the river. To his delight he sees his friend Mr. Pug, off for a day's fishing. Breathlessly the little bear pours out his story. "A Baby Badger floating down the river?" says Mr. Pug. "It sounds impossible. Come on. We mustn't lose a second or he may be right downstream."

Reaching the river beyond the gorge, Rupert is delighted to find that they are not too late. "There is the pram," he cries,."floating slowly towards us." Hurriedly Mr. Pug fits his rod together and puts on a large hook. Then he makes half a dozen casts, until the hook catches in the leather of the pram. Steadily the strange catch is pulled against the flow of the stream until they can grab at the handle.

RUPERT FINDS FOOTPRINTS

They land the pram and get a scare,
For Baby Badger isn't there.

Says Mr. Pug, "The footbridge cross;
Find someone to explain the loss."

Along the footbridge Rupert flies,
And through the hedge a gap he spies;

Then footprints down the bank appear,
And Baby's cry strikes Rupert's ear.

Dragging the pram up on to the rough and reedy shore, Mr. Pug lifts the blankets inside and both he and Rupert gaze in bewilderment. Baby Badger isn't there! "He must have fallen into the river," groans Mr. Pug.

"No," decides Rupert. "He was strapped in. Someone must have taken him—but how?" "Try the other bank," says Mr. Pug. "There's a foot-bridge near here. I'll see if there is any gap in the gorge this side."

Rupert scampers over the footbridge to explore the other side.

Footmarks point both ways, and while he is trying to solve what has happened a sudden noise makes him turn his head. "That was the cry of a Baby Badger," he gasps.

Rupert and Baby Badger

RUPERT IS CAPTURED

He runs and sees a caravan,
And close beside it stands a man,

The man, who's rough, grabs Rupert Bear,
And says, "I've caught you! Get in there."

The Man has got the Baby too,
And Rupert wonders what to do.

A chink of light shows through the floor,
So Rupert stoops the chink to explore.

Running in the direction of the cry, Rupert reaches a clearing and is confronted by a rough-looking man. Further away the man's wife is taking the Baby Badger into a caravan.

"Here," shouts Rupert, "that baby! What are you——?" but the man seizes him before he can finish. "If you can't mind your own business you must take the consequence," he growls, and thrusting the little bear into the caravan after the Badger Baby, he slams the doors.

"I wish I knew which direction we are taking," he thinks, peering out into the forest. Feverishly he tugs at the windows, but they are securely wedged, and he and the baby are prisoners. Then his eye catches a chink of light through the floor boards. "That board looks pretty rotten," he mutters.

RUPERT ESCAPES

He breaks the rotten board with haste,
Then grasps the Baby round the waist,

And bravely slithers to the ground,
While rumbling wheels disguise the sound.

The Countryside he doesn't know,
And wants to ask which way to go,

But not a single house is near,
And then a fog augments his fear.

An idea for escape suddenly strikes Rupert. Tugging at the rotten plank, he manages to pull it from its fastenings. Then he finds that a longer plank next to it is loose and he drags that away, the clattering of the wheels drowning the noise he makes.

When all is ready he sits on the edge of the hole he has made, with the Baby Badger in his arms, holds his breath and drops to the ground. He rolls on his back so that the axle shall not hit the baby, and they are free!

Picking himself up, Rupert is relieved to find that he has nothing worse than a bruise or two. Clasping the baby, he dodges behind some bushes and then pauses to try to get his bearings, but the country is quite strange to him. "We must find someone," he says to himself, "and ask the way to Nutwood."

RUPERT HEARS A VOICE

"I must sit down," at length he sighs,
And Baby, feeling chilly, cries.

But soon a woman comes their way,
And takes them to her hut to stay.

Says Rupert, "Homeward I must go,
So will you please the pathway show?"

He hurries on with cautious tread,
Then sees some car lights just ahead.

At length Rupert, quite exhausted, puts the Baby Badger on a rock and sits down in despair. The baby, not liking the fog, begins to cry lustily. "Now I simply don't know what to do," sighs the poor little bear.

All at once he is startled to see a dark figure looming up through the mist. "What's that baby doing out in the fog?" asks a kindly voice. "My hut is quite near, bring him there at once." It is an old countrywoman, and Rupert is only too thankful to follow her along a very muddy path.

"I must get back to tell Mr. Badger what has happened," says Rupert when they reach the hut. The countrywoman tells him the general direction and promises to keep the baby safe and warm until his return.

RUPERT TELLS HIS STORY

It's Mr. Porker, Rupert's friend,
Who's very pleased his help to lend,

Once home, brave Rupert runs pell-mell
To tell the Badgers all is well.

"A blunder," Rupert says, "I've made;
I'd better ask the Wise Goat's aid."

He asks the Goat, "What shall I do?"
The Goat says, "First, we want a clue."

To Rupert's great delight the motorist is his old friend, Mr. Porker. He readily offers the little bear a lift and very slowly they make for Nutwood. Near the village he puts him down and points the way to Mr. Badger's home.

Rupert's luck has now quite changed. As he enters the village the fog drifts away and there he sees Mr. Badger and Bill and Mr. Pug all looking very worried. "O my, won't they be glad to get my news," thinks Rupert, as he breaks into a run.

The little group stand bewildered. "Can't you remember any landmark?" asks Mr. Badger. "I only know it was a very long way," he sighs, "and I don't suppose anyone here knows the old country-woman, unless . . ."—suddenly he brightened—"the wise old goat! He knows more than any of us."

RUPERT ASKS MR. GOAT

As Rupert leaves, he hears a shout,
"Come back!   This plan may help you out."

The mud from Rupert's boot he takes;
Thinks Rupert, "What strange plans he makes!"

"Round here there's just one bit of ground
Where mud of such a kind is found;

That's where the hut is," says the Goat,
"I'll write directions in a note."

The wise old goat thinks deeply and then shakes his head. "There are many old countrywomen," he says slowly. "There is little to indicate which one has the Baby Badger." Sadly Rupert turns to go, when a shout arrests him. "Come here," says the wise one. "I've a notion that I may solve the mystery."

Spreading a paper over his knees, he takes a knife and starts carefully scraping the mud from one of Rupert's boots. "Whatever is he up to now?" thinks the little bear.

While Rupert watches in surprise the wise old goat carries the earth to a table and looks at it intently through a glass. "As I thought," he says at length, "there is only one place round here where that kind of earth is found."

RUPERT GETS A RIDE

For Rupert Bill sets out to wait;
He's standing just beside the gate;

And when the note Bill's father reads,
Straight to the hut the party speeds.

They find the hut and scramble out,
And Rupert gives a joyful shout.

The Baby's there quite safe and sound;
Oh, aren't they happy he's been found!

Taking Rupert to another room he points to a map. "You were there," he declares, "and the countrywoman's hut must be in that wood!" Then he writes instructions on a piece of paper and gives it to the little bear. Mr. Badger loses no time when he hears the news, and soon his little two-seater, with Rupert and Bill on board, is whizzing along the road with no trace of fog to hinder them.

At length the car reaches the wood and there, quite near the road, they spy the hut. In another moment Mr. Badger has his baby in his arms and thankfully he rewards the old countrywoman for her kindness.

"Good old Rupert!" cries Bill. "I don't know what would happen if I hadn't you to get me out of my scrapes!"

RUPERT

and the

MYSTERY

POND

Telling how Rupert
meets a stranger and
helps to solve the
mystery of the pond

RUPERT MEETS A STRANGER

Here's Rupert asking leave to play
With Bill, and Mother says he may.

He starts at once, and just beyond,
A stranger gazes in a pond.

Now when the little Bear's nearby,
The stranger curtly calls out "Hi!"

"I'd like you, please, to rack your brain,
And this mysterious stream explain."

It's such a long time since I saw my pal Bill Badger," says Rupert, one morning. "May I see if I can find him?" Mrs. Bear tells him not to get lost, and off he goes. Up on the common he approaches a little pond and sees a strange-looking little man standing by the edge of the water. "I've certainly never seen him before," thinks the little bear. "I wonder what he is doing round here?"

"Hi," says the strange little man, "I'm trying to solve some mysteries about this place; can you help me?" "Surely there aren't any mysteries," says Rupert. In reply, the other walks him round the pond to where a rapid stream flows out of it. "There," says the man, "what about that? How can such a lot of water flow out of the pond when there's nothing flowing in the other end?"

RUPERT SUSPECTS A SECRET

As Rupert hears this odd request,
The stranger measures round his chest,

And while the tape the man rewinds
A curious stick young Rupert finds.

Just as he's pondering what to say
The stick is roughly snatched away.

And while he wonders what is wrong
The man goes angrily along.

While Rupert is standing puzzled, the other suddenly produces a tape-measure and passes it round the little bear's chest. "What an extraordinary thing to do!" thinks Rupert in great surprise. "What was that for?" The little man gives no explanation, and while he is waiting Rupert picks up the curious walking-stick which he has been using. "This is most mysterious, too," he mutters."

For a while Rupert stands and studies the curious markings on the head of the walking-stick. Then it is snatched roughly from his hands. "That stick is old and valuable and those marks are secret," says the man, as he turns and stalks away irritably. "Well," gasps Rupert, "what is the meaning of it all? First the pond, and then the tape measure, and now the stick. What can there be secret about a walking stick?"

RUPERT MEETS BILL BADGER

Then, suddenly, upon a hill
There stands young Rupert's old friend, Bill.

With arms outstretched they start to run,
And Bill asks Rupert what he's done.

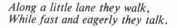

Along a little lane they walk,
While fast and eagerly they talk.

Quite soon, to their surprise they see
Some pram wheels. "Look!" they shout with glee.

Rupert goes on puzzling, but can make no sense of the things that have been happening, and he decides to give it up and continue his search for Bill Badger. Very soon from a little rise he spies his old pal! and they run to greet each other. "Oh, Rupert," cries Bill, "what a long time it is since I saw you. Where have you been? Do tell me what adventures you have been having."

The two pals wander along a little lane and Rupert tells Bill of the strange little man, but neither of them can understand him. All at once their attention is caught by something in the ditch beside them, and after groping about they pull up some old pram wheels. Forgetting about the strange man, Rupert studies them with interest. "They look quite strong," he says, "surely we could make something with these."

RUPERT BUILDS A TROLLEY

Then home the little wheels they take,
And there a trolley strong they make.

And Mrs. Bear comes out to see
Just how they mean to have a spree.

They shove the trolley down a slope;
But with it now they cannot cope;

The wheels are fixed, and soon the pair,
Are flung off madly in the air.

Running back to Nutwood with the old pram wheels, Rupert and Bill go straight to the shed in Mr. Bear's garden, where Rupert finds lots of useful wood and wire and nails. With these they build a trolley, fastening the axles on with strong wire. Then they show it proudly to Mrs. Bear, and Rupert stands on it to test it. Bill is all impatience to get out with it. "Let's take turns to pull each other over the common," he cries. Rupert and Bill have great fun pulling each other on their new trolley across the common. At length they come to the top of a long slope where they can sit down together, and in a moment they are gaining speed. Only then does Rupert realise with a shock that he cannot steer the trolley—both sets of wheels are fixed. To their dismay they cannot follow a bend in the path.

RUPERT HEARS CRIES

Down in some undergrowth they fall,
But out of it, unhurt, they crawl.

And as around the rocks they peer,
Bill cries, "Do hush! A voice I hear."

"Help, Help!" They hear some feeble cries,
And then they see a hand arise.

It is the stranger they have found;
He's hurt and can't get off the ground.

At the bottom of the slope Rupert's trolley turns right over, and the little pals are shot head first into some bushes. Picking themselves out gingerly, they find to their relief that they are not much hurt. Rupert runs to the trolley. "Look," he cries, "we made a jolly good job of this thing. It isn't damaged a bit!" But Bill holds up his hand for silence. "Hush," he whispers; "Did you hear that voice?

I believe someone is calling for help." Rupert listens, and sure enough feeble cries seem to be coming from some jumbled rocks. To Rupert's amazement they find the figure of the strange old explorer lying between two huge boulders. "Thank goodness you've come, little bear," says the man; "I slipped off a rock and badly hurt my ankle and thought I should never be found!"

RUPERT OFFERS TO SEARCH

They bring their trolley round the hill,
Then Rupert lifts, and so does Bill,

And up the stony, rough-hewn road
They safely pull their heavy load.

To Rupert Mr. Bear attends,
And for a doctor quickly sends;

While Rupert makes a bold request—
To solve the mystery for his guest.

Running to fetch their trolley, Rupert and Bill get on either side of the strange little man and help him to struggle on to it. It bears his weight, and soon they are manfully tugging him back uphill towards Nutwood. "My word," pants Rupert, "it's lucky for him that we had that accident when the trolley ran away and threw us into the bushes, or we should never have come this way at all!"

Mr. Bear is very surprised to see the little procession, and quickly invites the poor old explorer in and sends for a doctor. Later on, when his ankle is heavily bound up, Rupert and Bill approach the strange little man. "Please," says Rupert, "you won't be able to do any exploring for some time now. Won't you let us go to try to solve the mystery of that little pond for you?"

RUPERT LOOKS FOR CLUES

"Then take this stick," the old man cries;
"It gives the clue if you are wise."

They study words, and carving, too,
To make the stick reveal the clue.

They write the words, then have a chat;
" 'The Lake of Nutwood'; where is that?"

Says Bill, "let's have another ride;
Perhaps we'll get ideas outside."

The old man smiles at Rupert's question. "Very well," he says, "but I'm not going to tell you anything. You may borrow this valuable stick of mine. It is supposed to have all the clues to the mystery. If you can solve them you're very clever." Eagerly grasping the stick, Rupert and Bill study the strange carving on it. "Let's write it all down and see if it makes any sense," suggests Bill.

Getting some paper Rupert carefully puts down the signs from the walking stick. "First there was the 'Lake of Nutwood'," he says; "then there was a capital 'I', and an 'S', and then a thing that looks like a bell." They think hard, but can make nothing of it. "It's no good," says Bill, "there isn't a Lake of Nutwood, unless it means that mysterious little pond."

Rupert and the Mystery Pond

RUPERT STARTS THE SEARCH

Cries Rupert, "I.S.—south, one mile;
Let's give that clue a little trial."

So, finding south by weathervane,
They take their trolley out again.

They tramp along, and reach a wood,
And think this way can't be much good,

When Bill espies a curious light,
Set in a tree, and shining bright.

Rupert and Bill go back to their trolley. "Which direction shall we go?" asks Bill. "Direction?" says Rupert excitedly. "That's given me an idea! Do you think that the 'I S' on the stick could mean one mile south from Nutwood?" "My word, that's clever!" says Bill; "we've got no other clue, so we may as well try it and see where it leads us." Taking turns to pull each other on the trolley, the two little pals reach broken ground and find their way blocked by a thick forest. "Oh, dear," says Rupert in disappointment, "we can't go any further this way, and I don't know if we've come a mile or not. Perhaps my idea was wrong." They are sadly turning to retrace their steps when Bill suddenly grips his arm. "Look," he says, "what is that thing shining in the sunlight halfway up that tree?"

RUPERT FINDS THE BELL

They rush, excited, to the tree,
To find out what the light can be.

Bill climbs up first: shouts "Rupert, quick!
We're on the trail; do bring that stick."

Then Rupert, climbing, sees the bell
That's carved upon the stick as well.

He strikes the bell, out pops an owl;
"Hullo! Who's there?" they hear him growl.

Rupert and Bill run to discover what the shining thing is. As they near the tree the object, whatever it was, gets hidden by the foliage. Bill gets to the tree first and quickly climbs out of sight, while Rupert waits impatiently by the trolley. Then Bill returns and beckons. "Come up here, Rupert," he says in a strange voice, "and bring that queer stick with you." Clambering up to join Bill, Rupert is amazed to find a large, shining, silver bell hanging from a branch. "Why, this must be the bell marked on the stick!" he gasps; "but how can this possibly solve the mystery of Nutwood Lake? A lake can't be up a tree!" As he speaks he strikes the bell. Instantly there is a click, two little doors in the tree fly open, and a voice cries, "Who's there?" Turning in astonishment, they see an old owl sitting inside the trunk.

RUPERT FINDS THE STONE

He sees the stick and says, "Now you
Must keep on south, a stone's the clue."

And so the pair move on with haste;
They haven't any time to waste.

Their trolley they have left behind;
They simply want the stone to find.

At length they think they've reached their goal—
A stone that has a tiny hole.

Climbing round until they are facing the old owl, Rupert and Bill eagerly explain what they are searching for. "I see you are holding the ancient stick, therefore I can help you," says the bird. "Now, you must continue south until you reach the Three o'clock Stone. See if you can solve that clue." And without another word the owl disappears and the doors snap to. They scramble down in haste.

Leaving their trolley behind, Rupert and Bill run right through the forest. In a clearing on the other side they find a huge stone, quite round, rather like a great mushroom and with a little hole right in the middle of it. "This is the only queer stone we've seen," says Rupert, "but is it the stone we're seeking? And why did the owl call it the Three o'clock Stone?" "There's nothing to tell us," says Bill, very puzzled.

RUPERT HEARS THE CLOCK STRIKE

Now in this hole the stick they fit,
Then on the stone, perplexed, they sit.

Soon Bill gets up and walks about,
And all at once he gives a shout.

For now their stick's long shadow lies
Upon a stone of smaller size.

They lift it to investigate
And find a handled, iron plate.

For curiosity, Rupert puts the old stick into the little hole in the stone and finds it fits exactly. Then he and Bill sit down to think about it, but they can make no headway. Suddenly the clock in the village church below chimes three o'clock. "There must be some other clue," says Bill desperately as he gets up for a stroll.

Almost at once Rupert hears a shout from him and sees him pointing at the ground a little way off. The autumn sun is already low, and the shadow of of the stick is flung across the ground and points, just like an arrow, to the centre of another and smaller stone. Heaving the stone up, they see to their amazement that beneath it is a round iron plate with a handle. "Hooray," shouts Rupert, "this looks really exciting."

RUPERT DESCENDS THE PIT

.And there's a ladder leads below,
Down which brave Rupert says he'll go.

"The hole's so small," he shouts, "I've guessed
Why that old man sized up my chest."

Once down below he sees strange sights—
Caves, waterfalls, and greenish lights;

But when he turns his friend to call
He's lost, and can't get back at all.

When the iron plate is removed Rupert and Bill see a little iron ladder leading straight down a deep hole. Bill looks dubious. "Well, but Nutwood Lake cannot be down there," he says. But Rupert cannot resist trying the ladder. "My word," he says as he descends, "this hole is a tight fit." Then a strange thought strikes him. "I wonder," he mutters, "whether this is why that strange old man measured me."

Rupert descends many yards and finds himself in a very rough funnel. Waterfalls appear and drop into deep holes, and there is a strange greenish light everywhere. "Bill would like this. I'll tell him to come down," says the little bear. He turns round and tries to retrace his steps, but the passages divide in all directions and soon he realises to his dismay that he is lost.

RUPERT MEETS THE TOAD

He crawls on now, then there's a gleam;
He finds he's gazing in a stream.

And next a giant toad appears,
Who's seen no one in fifty years.

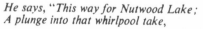

He says, "This way for Nutwood Lake;
A plunge into that whirlpool take,

And home you'll be in half a twink";
But Rupert feels his courage shrink.

Rupert realises there is nothing for it but to go on. He crawls through passages for over an hour before finding his way barred by an underground stream. As he pauses, a deep voice startles him. "Well, well," it booms, "a little bear! You're my first visitor for fifty years. How did you get here?" Rupert sees before him an extraordinary creature like a huge toad. Rapidly he explains his search.

"Please," he says, "I've been trying to find Nutwood Lake, but I'm afraid I'm lost!" "You're not lost at all," booms the giant toad as he moves a few yards away. "This is Nutwood Lake, and if you want to get back to Nutwood quickly you just drop straight in!" Below him the dark waters rush round at great speed, making a dangerous looking whirlpool.

RUPERT ENTERS THE WHIRLPOOL

He's told he'll have no time to drown,
So trustfully he plunges down,

And wonders where on earth he's gone,
As swirling waters sweep him on.

Then up he's flung at lightning speed,
While round him waggle tongues of weed.

And all at once, to his delight
He's in a pond, in sunshine bright.

"You'd never find your way back as you came," says the huge toad. "As I said before, you'd better go into the whirlpool. You'll be all right. You won't have time to drown." The toad will tell him no more, so at last the little bear decides to trust his word and risk it. Holding his breath, he plunges straight into the middle of the swirling water. In an instant he is dragged down and swept through a narrow space between great rocks. After being dragged down a long way Rupert finds the direction changes and he is shot upwards at equal speed. Then the speed lessens, his head suddenly breaks surface, and to his joy he can breathe again. Quickly he splashes and struggles to the grassy bank and sees that he is now in a little pond with no houses in sight.

RUPERT MEETS THE SEARCH PARTY

He looks about him, dripping wet,
And says, "Why, here the man I met;

"And look, there's father, Bill, the twins!
They're searching for me," Rupert grins.

He shouts, "I'm back, I've had such fun,"
And starts to tell what he has done.

But Mr. Bear says, "Home you fly,
We'll hear your story when you're dry."

Running round the pond, Rupert pauses as he reaches the stream that flows out of it. Something about it seems familiar. "Why," he shouts, "this is where I met that strange explorer man. And to think that I've solved the problem of where all this water comes from." Happily he runs towards Nutwood, and is delighted to see Bill Badger leading Mr. Bear and the Rabbit twins over the common.

Shouting as he runs, Rupert joins the little search party. "Oh, Rupert," says Bill, "we thought you were lost for ever! When you didn't come back I took the stick and our trolley to Nutwood, and we were just off to look for you." In great excitement Rupert begins to tell his story. "You are still soaking wet," says Mr. Bear. "Home you go before you catch your death of cold, and we'll hear the story later."

RUPERT SOLVES THE PROBLEM

And Mrs. Bear says, "Gracious me!
A bath's the thing for you, I see."

Says Rupert, sitting in the steam,
"I've solved the mystery of the stream."

The old explorer, now quite well,
Enjoys the tale he has to tell

And says, "Because you found the Lake
My stick, as a remembrance, take."

Rupert runs into Nutwood at top speed. Mrs. Bear is horrified to see how wet he is, and quickly hurries him indoors and pops him into a hot bath. Rupert still pours out his story, and asks where the old explorer is. "He's still here," says Mrs. Bear. "His ankle is better, and he'll soon be going. You shall go down and see him directly." "He'll be excited to know I've solved his problem," chuckles the little bear. Sure enough the strange old man is better and is very surprised to hear Rupert's story. "I should never have got down that hole," he smiles. "I'm much too fat. Now my exploring round here is finished." Giving Rupert his curious stick as a keepsake, he says good-bye. "I suppose we shall never know who he was," says the little bear.

RUPERT
and the
FOREST
FIRE

Rupert meets another
inventor and solves
the mystery of the
smoke in the forest

RUPERT HEARS OF FIRE

The birds seek Rupert's help to obtain,
So one taps on the window-pane,

And Mr. Crow, with frightened croak,
Says "Help! the forest's full of smoke!"

Then Rupert seeks his father's aid,
And he calls up the Fire Brigade,

While Rupert rushes towards the fire,
Where smoke's ascending ever higher.

One morning a curious noise brings Rupert to the window. A little bird is beating at the glass and is evidently trying to attract attention. Running outside, Rupert is surprised to find a collection of birds of all sizes flying round wildly. "O, Rupert," cries a large crow, "can you do anything to help us? The forest is full of smoke. It must be on fire, we shall lose all our nests!"

"How dreadful!" cries the little bear. "I'll tell my daddy at once!" Hurrying to find his father and tell him of the fire, Rupert points through the window, and, sure enough, the sky is beginning to fill with smoke. "I'll go and 'phone for the fire brigade," declares Mr. Bear. While he goes to the village Rupert decides that he may as well go to the forest himself.

RUPERT INVESTIGATES

Some birds fly back, afraid they'll choke,
But Rupert hurries through the smoke.

Then, greatly puzzled, he exclaims,
"Why, Mr. Crow, where are the flames?"

With handkerchief he guards his nose,
As through the thickening smoke he goes,

And comes at last upon a briar,
Which pours out smoke without a fire.

After climbing the hill Rupert enters the forest. One by one the birds drop out until only the big crow is left. At length they stop. "I can't go any further," says the crow. "We'd better turn back." But Rupert is puzzled. "There is a lot of smoke," he says, "but where's it coming from? I can't hear any roaring or crackling. Where are the flames? I've a good mind to look further into this!"

Rupert is as good as his word. Breathing through his handkerchief so as not to choke, he pushes on, always going where the smoke is thickest. He comes all at once upon a great tangled briar out of which dense masses of smoke are pouring and which is evidently the source of the trouble. He gazes at it in bewilderment. The bush should have been all burnt up long ago.

RUPERT FINDS A CHIMNEY

All scratched and torn the briar he breaks,
And through its thorns his way he makes.

And there he finds a chimney round,
That flings up smoke from underground.

He's nearly choked as back he flies,
To tell the birds of this surprise.

They thank him, but, while smoke infests
The trees, they cannot use their nests.

Rupert is determined to solve the mystery. He gets scratched and his clothes are torn, but at length he reaches a clear space right in the middle, and there, sticking up out of the ground, is a great metal chimney through which the smoke is pouring. "Good gracious!" gasps the little bear. "Where on earth does that lead to? There must be a great fire down underground right in the middle of the hill."

He decides to go back and ask his friends the birds. Outside the forest he finds the birds still twittering in excitement, and he tells them all about the strange chimney, but none of them seems to know anything about any underground furnace. "It's jolly clever of you to have found out that the forest isn't on fire at all," says the crow, "but we aren't much better off yet."

Rupert and the Forest Fire

RUPERT SCENTS A MYSTERY

While wondering what the smoke reveals,
Young Rupert finds the trace of wheels.

At once he hides and keeps quite still,
For something's coming round the hill.

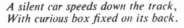

A silent car speeds down the track,
With curious box fixed on its back.

So Rupert, puzzled, asks the crow,
"Whose car?" The old bird doesn't know.

At the foot of the slope the little bear pauses suddenly. "Those wheel tracks," he says, "I'm sure they weren't there when we entered the wood. Why should anything drive along over the grass in this lonely spot?" All at once Rupert dodges behind a tree and waits. Something has appeared round the hill, returning along those same tracks.

Peeping out from his hiding-place, Rupert sees that an odd-looking motor-car is approaching. It shoots past him at a good speed. "What an extraordinary motor!" mutters Rupert. "There isn't a sound from the engine, and I wonder what that round box affair at the back is." Once again the crow can't give him any information. "I see most things round here," declares the bird, "but I've never seen that thing before."

RUPERT FINDS THE CAR

To solve the mystery he gives chase,
But with the car he can't keep pace.

The tracks direct him to some stones,
And there they're lost; poor Rupert groans.

For quite a while he searches round,
Then hears nearby a crunching sound.

He spies a hillside hole, then jumps,
For out of it that motor bumps.

His curiosity gets the better of him and he dashes after the motor, which, however, gains on him and disappears round another bend of the hill. Rupert has the wheel marks to guide him. At length he is led to a lot of bushes, and to his disappointment the grass gives way to a stretch of stones and boulders, where, of course, the tracks do not show.

Rupert searches all round to try to pick up the wheel tracks of the strange motor, but without success. He is about to turn round and go home when he notices an extra thick clump of bush, and as he approaches he hears, to his excitement, a sound of crunching beyond it. Peering through the branches he sees, to his surprise, a great hole in the hill below him and out of it shoots the queer car he has been following.

RUPERT IS CAUGHT

He scrambles down and finds a cave,
And then, because he's very brave,

He goes inside; steel coils he finds,
A bench, and tools of many kinds.

He hears the car again outside;
Poor Rupert! There's no time to hide.

The driver, looking most severe,
Grabs him and shouts, "What's brought you here?"

"It's no good trying to follow that car again: it goes too fast for me," thinks Rupert. "I'm going to explore this strange place it came from." Descending quietly, he screws up his courage and enters through the doorway into a great cave that goes straight into the middle of the hill. To his surprise the inside is got up like a workshop. There is a great bench, lots of tools and boxes of equipment, and, queerest of all, several huge coils of steel. Rupert is so interested by the things in the cave workshop that he forgets how long he has been there. Then he gasps as he realises he is too late. The car comes straight inside the hill and he is caught. The driver stops near him and, leaping out, grabs Rupert's arm. "Now then, what are you doing here?" he demands. "Who are you?"

Rupert and the Forest Fire

RUPERT SEES THE FIRE

Rupert explains, then with amaze,
He sees a glowing furnace blaze.

It's there to make an all-steel car,
And flings its smoke up high and far.

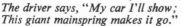

The driver says, "My car I'll show;
This giant mainspring makes it go."

Then Rupert says, "How kind you've been!
Good-bye, and thanks for all I've seen."

Rupert quickly explains that he has been meaning no harm, and to his surprise and relief the driver seems to get less fierce. "Come along," says the man, "I'm inventing an entirely new kind of car and making it all steel," revealing a raging fire behind. "Why!" shouts Rupert in excitement, "that solves my first mystery. It must be your fire here that sends all that smoke up through the chimney in the forest up above. The birds thought the forest was on fire!" Next, the driver shows Rupert the car. "This is a clockwork car. Inside that round thing is a giant mainspring which you just wind up with that handle and the car goes for hours at no cost." Rupert is thrilled. "How perfectly topping!" he says. "That explains those great coils of steel I saw in your workshop, and it explains why your car is so queer—no noise from the engine."

RUPERT IS CAPTURED

The man replies, "You go? No fear!
You've learned my secrets, you'll stay here!"

He leads him up a staircase long;
"Oh dear," thinks Rupert, "what's gone wrong?"

The fickle man wears quite a frown,
As rocky paths they hurry down.

And Rupert gives a weary groan,
As in the cave he's left alone.

To Rupert's dismay the man doesn't shake hands, and he looks at the little bear with a curious expression. "Oh, no," he smiles, "I'm afraid I can't say good-bye to you. Now that you have found out my secrets you must remain here until my experiments are done and the car is perfect. I can't risk letting you go!" And, taking Rupert firmly by the hand, he leads him through other doorways and up steps and into passages until the little bear is bewildered and wonders where he will end up.

At length the man reaches a passage so low that he has to bend down to get through. "These used to be mine workings," he says as he leads Rupert to a lonely cavern at the other end. "Nobody usually comes here, and I took them over hoping not to be discovered. I'm afraid you must stay here."

Rupert and the Forest Fire

RUPERT MEETS FRIEND MOUSE

"Now how can I get out?" he cries,
"I know," a little mouse replies.

And leads him to an old trap-door,
Which Rupert hadn't seen before.

So on the handle Rupert hauls;
The door gives way and down he falls.

The driver startled, hurried round,
To see what caused that crashing sound.

Rupert finds that his cavern is a very odd-shaped one with branches in all directions, but he can find no other way out than the one by which he came. Suddenly a voice by his ear squeaks. "Do you want to get out? I'll show you how." Turning quickly, he sees a friendly looking mouse, and, following the little creature, finds himself looking at an old trap-door.

Thanking the friendly little mouse, Rupert steps over to the trap-door and bends down to lift it. To his horror the wood is so old that it collapses and he tumbles right through to another cave below. His fall is broken, but it makes an awful crash, and in a minute the driver appears looking very startled. "Good gracious!" he cries. "I forgot that old trap-door up there."

Rupert *and the Forest Fire*

RUPERT HAS A RIDE

"Perhaps to shut you up was wrong,"
The driver says, "so come along;

When I have tightened up this screw,
I'll test the car, and you'll come, too.

"Now watch to see that nut holds tight,
Or else the spring won't keep in right."

But Rupert quickly gets the jumps,
Because the motor shakes and bumps.

The driver seems to be very relieved that Rupert is not hurt by his fall. "Perhaps I was wrong to shut you up," he says. "It would be better to get you to help with the trials of my new car. I could still keep you under my eye, so that you couldn't give away any of my secrets." This idea suits Rupert, and he readily agrees.

Before starting, the man gives Rupert his in-struction. "I've got my strongest spring inside that case," he says. "Your job will be to keep an eye on it. If that nut on top looks like coming off you must tell me at once and I'll stop immediately. It's very important." Rupert finds that the only way he can do it properly is by sitting on the back of the seat. It doesn't feel safe and he is very worried as the car starts bumping its way out of the cave.

RUPERT IS FLUNG OUT

It bounces madly over stones;
"Oh dear, I'll fall," poor Rupert groans.

And then he gets a ghastly scare
The nut goes flying through the air.

Poor Rupert makes a fateful move,
Just as the spring leaps from its groove;

Now in his clothes the steel gets wound,
And so he's wildly whirled around.

As the car reaches open country it gains speed and bounces terribly over the rough land. Poor Rupert has such difficulty in holding on to his awkward perch that he doesn't notice that the great nut before him is being jolted loose. At last, as they bump over an extra big stone, the nut flies off before his face. He yells to the driver to stop, but it is too late. In an instant the case of the mainspring starts coming to pieces. In his fright at what has happened Rupert makes a despairing leap away from the case and the driver tries frantically to stop the car, but it is all too late. Another jolt and the powerful spring snaps out of its groove, the end catches under Rupert's sweater, and the little bear is whisked high into the air and whirled round and round at a terrific speed.

RUPERT FEELS LOST

Into a tree at length he lands,
And catches hold with both his hands.

He scrambles down, and from the tree,
The car in water he can see.

The driver, very wet, climbs out,
And Rupert, breathless, tries to shout;

The man can't hear and hurries on,
"I'm lost," sighs Rupert. "Where's he gone?"

Being swung round so fast makes Rupert very giddy. When he comes to his senses he finds he has been flung into the upper branches of a tall tree. Gingerly he moves and realises to his relief that he is not much hurt. Cautiously he starts descending, and when half-way down he looks round for signs of the strange car. To his consternation he sees that the driver must have lost control, for the car is now stuck in the middle of a pond. Completing his descent, Rupert hurries to the pond in time to see the driver, very wet and dishevelled, scramble out on the other side and stride away. He shouts to attract his attention, but the little bear is still breathless from his experience with the mainspring and his voice is not very loud. The man doesn't hear and quickly disappears from sight.

RUPERT MEETS THE CROW

Now Rupert's tale two rabbits hear,
And tell him that his home's quite near.

They find the mainspring on the way.
"A dangerous thing," the rabbits say.

A lorry past the forest drives,
When Rupert near his home arrives.

He seeks the cave the man to find;
It's empty! Nothing's left behind.

While Rupert watches the car it sinks out of sight. A couple of rabbits arrive to see what is happening, and Rupert explains his troubles. "Ah," says one of them, "that pond has a soft, muddy floor. You'll never see that car again. If you want to return to Nutwood it isn't far across country. We'll show you the way." At length Rupert comes in sight of the forest which he thought had been on fire. A lorry is driving past the foot of the hill and the smoke had nearly gone. As he runs his friend the crow rejoins him, and together they make for the cave. To his amazement it is now deserted. "That driver must have changed his plans when he lost his car," says Rupert. "He's taken all his tools and things away, probably in that lorry I saw. I do hope he won't have any more accidents when he starts his experiments again."

RUPERT GOES HOME

While Rupert tells the crow his tale,
The firemen come upon the trail.

So Rupert takes them to the briar,
To prove there was no forest fire.

The firemen gladly wave good-bye,
While happy birds around them fly;

And Rupert's parents smile with glee,
To see their son safe home for tea.

As they reach the wood there is a shout and up rush some firemen. "Good gracious, you have been a long time!" cries Rupert. Then he smiles. "Anyway, there never was a forest fire," he chuckles. The firemen don't understand, so he leads them through the trees right into the middle of the briar bush, where the strange chimney leading from the cave below is sticking up out of the ground, and he tells them all that has happened. Then the birds make a fuss of him for putting out the forest fire. "I seem to be getting a lot of credit for doing nothing," says Rupert. "I didn't put out the fire and I didn't do that poor driver much good!" But the birds insist on making him their hero and a crowd of them accompany him across the common.

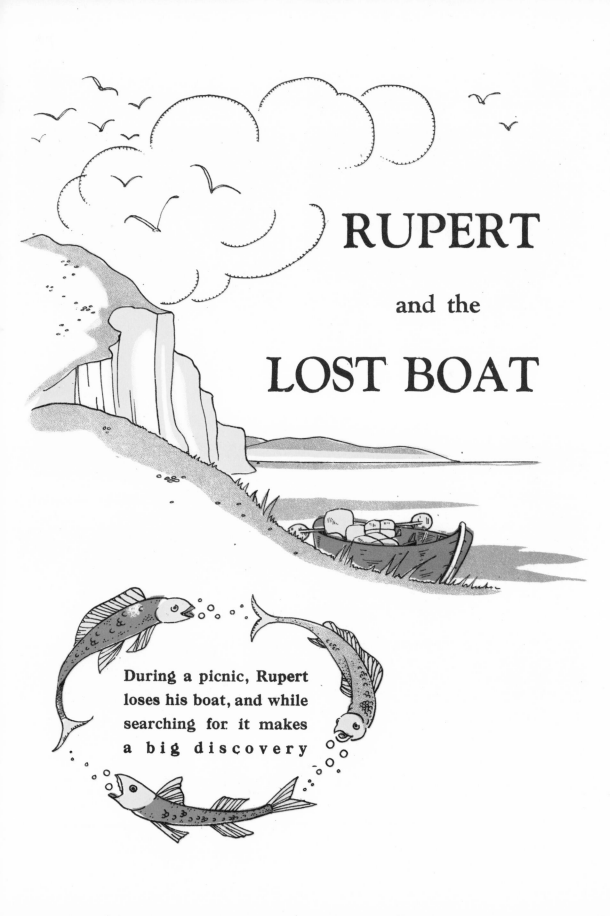

RUPERT

and the

LOST BOAT

During a picnic, Rupert
loses his boat, and while
searching for it makes
a big discovery

RUPERT GETS A WARNING

Says Rupert, "Algy, come with me;
Let's go by river to the sea."

Provisions and a tent they pack,
And stop near trees to have a snack.

The wood's so nice they plan to stay,
And camp there for at least a day.

But then a talking rabbit cries,
"You won't remain here, if you're wise."

Rupert and Algy the Pug are off on a new kind of holiday. Into Rupert's tiny boat they have piled a folding tent and their haversacks and lots of provisions, and they are trying to get right down the river to the seaside. Algy points ashore. "Look," he cries, "there's a topping wood on that bank. Do let's pull in there and have lunch." Once ashore, Rupert and Algy pitch their camp. Rupert ties the boat to a tree stump while Algy hauls the tent and their haversacks ashore; then they drag all the gear to a sheltered glade in the bushes. "What are you two doing here?" asks a voice, and a large rabbit appears in front of them. "This is no place for strangers. I advise you to clear off as quickly as you can." Rupert is very surprised. "No fear," he says cheerfully, "we are going to camp here."

RUPERT MEETS THE OWNER

They won't believe, and start to eat,
When there's a sound of trampling feet.

The rabbit bolts, the others peep
And towards their boat see someone creep.

Says Algy, "We were mad to stay
Let's hurry up and run away."

But Rupert says, "No, let's explain,"
And so he tries, but all in vain.

Rupert and Algy sit down happily to eat their lunch, but the rabbit is very worried, and looks at them anxiously. "You don't understand," he says: "the owner of this land is a very cantankerous man." Breaking off, he suddenly bolts down his burrow. There is the sound of someone moving near them. Creeping silently towards the noise, Rupert and Algy peep around a bush and see a strange man walking towards their boat. Algy wants to run away, but Rupert says, "No, we must go to him and explain about the boat," and, screwing up his courage, he leads the way forward. "Please," says Rupert, "this looked such a lovely wood we thought we should like to stay here for a bit." To his dismay, the man only scowls the more and advances angrily to seize them.

RUPERT TAKES ADVICE

The man picks up the luckless pair,
And hurries off with frightening glare.

And then, with anger most intense,
He hurls them both across a fence.

A blackbird whistles, "If you're wise,
You'll do just what I now advise."

"Take this short cut—and mind you hide!
You'll find then where your boat is tied."

Rupert still tries to say how sorry he is, but the man gives him no chance. Seizing the two chums firmly he marches away from the river until he reaches the edge of the wood. Then he puts them roughly over a fence and shakes his fist. "That'll teach you to come where you're not wanted," he shouts and, turning round, he strides away.

Rupert's first thought is to get back to the tent and to the boat, but he and Algy are afraid to enter the wood for fear of meeting the man again. As they are pondering a big blackbird alights on the fence and they tell him their troubles. "Your best way is to take a short cut to the river and then follow the stream until you reach your boat," he advises. Then he gives them full directions, and soon Rupert and Algy are moving cautiously along the river bank.

RUPERT TRACES THE BOAT

But when they reached their landing-place,
The boat has gone and left no trace.

They search awhile without avail,
Then Algy comes upon a trail.

Although their hearts beat loud with fear,
They follow where the trail is clear,

And reach at length a padlocked store;
Their boat shows through a splintered door.

After a long walk following the winding bank of the river, Rupert and Algy reach the spot where they had landed. There an unpleasant surprise awaits them, for, to their horror, their boat has gone! "Look, Algy," he calls, "something has been dragged out of the river and across the grass here. It must be our boat and that man must have stolen it!" Sure enough the trail leads away into the depths of the wood.

Rupert and Algy at first follow the trail of the boat. All at once a large shed appears in sight and the trail leads straight to the large doors. After making sure that their enemy is not there, they go forward. "The boat is inside," whispers Rupert excitedly, peering through a crack in the door. "Yes," says Algy, "but that's not much use to us while these doors are shut—just look at that huge padlock."

RUPERT DECIDES TO HIDE

"Now, Algy," Rupert says, "stand by,
While I to find some help will try."

But soon he hears a frightened shout,
"That man is coming! Quick! Look out!"

"Come on!" says Rupert, "follow me!
And we can hide up in this tree."

They shelter in the leaves so green,
And watch the man come on the scene.

"That man has locked up our boat—we must get it back," says Rupert. "I tell you what, I'll run for help and you must hide near here to watch if he comes to move the boat away again." The little bear has gone only a short way when he hears Algy dashing after him. "Oh," gasps Algy as he approaches, "that dreadful man. He saw me before I saw him and now he's chasing me."

Rupert realises there isn't a moment to lose if their enemy isn't to catch them again. "Come on—straight up this tree," he calls urgently. Leading the way, he helps Algy up to a strong branch and, while they lie there panting, they see the man run into the clearing and gaze about. Hardly daring to breathe, the **two** pals see him pause irresolutely under the very branch on which they are hiding.

Rupert and the Lost Boat

RUPERT FOLLOWS ALGY

*He's looking round among the trees
When Algy gives a fearful sneeze,*

*And falling, knocks the man right down;
"You're caught!" the man cries with a frown.*

*Poor Algy's led off in a fright,
And Rupert follows, out of sight.*

*Inside a house, with windows barred,
He sees his friend go, under guard.*

Rupert and Algy wait in silence while their enemy stands beneath the tree, and then a terrible thing happens. Algy feels a sneeze coming on! He sneezes suddenly and violently and rolls off the branch right on to the head of the man beneath. Rupert up aloft watches helplessly, wondering what will happen next. "So I've caught you again," growls the man. "This time you shall learn your lesson!"

More angry than ever the man marches Algy away while Rupert carefully descends the tree. "It's no use my trying to rescue Algy by myself," thinks he unhappily, "we should both be locked up, and then where should we be?" Keeping well out of sight he trails the man until he finds himself in a clearing and in front of a square, forbidding house into which poor Algy is being hustled.

RUPERT LISTENS TO RABBIT

"Now," Rupert thinks, "how to set him free!"
Then sees an overhanging tree.

"Our tent rope I will fetch," he cries;
Alas, it's gone. "We're lost," he sighs.

The friendly rabbit, standing near,
Says, "All your things were seized, I fear;

But Rupert, please don't give up hope,
I'll tell you where to buy some rope."

Rupert prowls cautiously round the house, and in a few moments Algy's head appears at one of the upper windows. Then an idea strikes him. "Look at that tree," he mutters; "with a piece of rope I could rescue him on to one of those branches." He runs back to the glade where they had meant to pitch their camp. There is nothing there. The tent, the haversacks, the food—everything has gone!

"Are you searching for your haversacks and things?" says the rabbit. "That man came and took them all away." "Oh, dear," groans Rupert, "I must get some rope." He sits down in despair. "Cheer up," says the rabbit; "why not buy some rope? There is a village here."

And he then gives Rupert careful directions how to get there.

RUPERT FINDS HALF-A-CROWN

So Rupert, who has half-a-crown,
To purchase rope runs to the town.

But near the fence a half-crown lies;
"I wonder who dropped that," he cries.

Till Algy's rescued, he can't stop,
And dashes on into the shop,

He hands, in haste, the new half-crown
The shopman greets it with a frown.

"I have half-a-crown of my own," he says. "I wonder if that would be enough for a strong rope." And he sets off at a good speed. At the edge of the wood something shining in the grass catches his eye. He gets back and picks it up. It is another half-crown—a bright new one. "Now, who can have dropped that?" he mutters.

Slipping it into his pocket he runs on and soon has found the village shop. To his delight he sees some coils of rope hanging up, and asks the shopman for one. At the same time he produces a half-crown and hands it over the counter. Then there is a pause, and to his surprise the shopman turns the coin over and over and scowls at it. "What's the matter with the man?" thinks the little bear; "why doesn't he let me have my rope?"

RUPERT GETS A FRIGHT

"Be off!" he hears the shopman shout,
"There's lots of these bad coins about."

He calls a policeman, who's outside,
And Rupert slips off, terrified.

To Algy's prison back he goes;
And with each step his panic grows.

Then, hiding near the house, he spies
The man go out. "That's good," he cries.

To Rupert's amazement the shopman comes from behind his counter and hustles him out of the shop. "Get away from here," he shouts, "that was a bad half-crown. There have been dozens of them about lately—I wish I could catch the man who is making them. Be off with you!" Rupert tries to explain things, but the man angrily turns to call a policeman, and, feeling by now very frightened, Rupert decides that his best plan is to make good his escape. Reaching the strange house where Algy is imprisoned he crouches in the shrubbery. He is only just in time. Footsteps are heard and his enemy appears, walking rapidly away from the house. "Come, that's better," thinks Rupert. "If that dreadful man goes away for a while I may be able to talk to Algy and find out how the land lies."

RUPERT CLIMBS A TREE

He climbs a tree and calls his chum,
And Algy cries, "I'm glad you've come."

Along a bough, to reach his friend,
Brave Rupert crawls, but feels it bend.

He's just about to jump when—crack!
He hits the roof upon his back.

And now, how can he get inside?
A skylight he will open wide.

When the man has disappeared Rupert rapidly scrambles up the tree which is opposite Algy's window. At his shout the little Pug appears. "Oh, Rupert," he calls joyfully, "how glad I am to see you!" "There's just one chance," says Rupert. "One of the branches stretches over the house and I may reach you that way."

Just as Rupert is thinking of jumping down to the parapet there is a sharp crack and, still clinging to the end of the bough, he drops with a bump on to the tiles. The rest of the branch flies back to its original position, now well out of reach. Rupert picks himself up and gazes upward ruefully. "Well, I can't get back again that way," he sighs. "I must try to enter the house and reach Algy. What about these skylights?"

RUPERT MEETS ALGY

A crowded attic room he sees,
And steps, down which he runs with ease.

Then, hearing cooped-up Algy shout,
He cries, "Cheer up! I'll get you out."

The next room's open, he looks round,
And sees the walls are quite unsound.

By tugging hard he makes a breach,
And so his playmate he can reach.

With much puffing and pushing Rupert manages to fasten the skylight open and finds himself peeping into a tiny attic. From it a ladder leads down through a hole in the floor. He carefully descends the ladder to reach behind one of the doors, and running to it he turns the handle. The door is locked and the key has been taken away. "Cheer up, Algy," cries the little bear, "I'll explore the other rooms."

In the room next to Algy's, Rupert is struck by the broken-down state of the house. "H'm, there's not much here to help me to get Algy out," he thinks. Then his eye brightens. "Those bricks look rotten," he murmurs. "I do believe I could pull them out." Running to the wall he tugs at the loose pieces, and to Algy's great delight there is soon such a large hole that Rupert can put his head through to greet his pal.

Rupert and the Lost Boat

RUPERT FINDS THE COINS

They make the opening nice and wide,
And Algy's soon at Rupert's side.

Then, creeping down a narrow stair,
They come on some machinery rare.

Says Rupert, "What a strange machine!
But hurry up, don't let's be seen."

"Here!" Algy cries, "just take a peep—
They're all half-crowns in this big heap."

In great excitement Algy helps with the removal of bricks until he is able to step through the next room and join Rupert. Together they creep downstairs on their way to freedom. "I do wish we knew where the man keeps the key of that shed," says Rupert. Keeping a wary look-out in case the man returns, Rupert rounds a corner and his attention is caught by a room full of odd machinery.

They can make nothing of it at first. "Come on, Algy, we mustn't waste too much time here," says Rupert, "the man may come back at any minute." "Half a mo'," says Algy in a strange voice, "come and look here." Running to his pal, the little bear finds him bending over a box. Then he, too, stands in amazement. Inside the box and in heaps all round it are thousands of new, shining half-crowns!

RUPERT TELLS THE POLICE

"I found," says Rupert, "near the trees,
A bad half-crown—quite new, like these."

"They're being made by that bad man;
Let's go and tell fast as we can."

They sprint along and never stop
Until they reach the village shop;

And how the police and shopman stare
When Rupert tells what brings them there!

Rupert quickly recovers from his astonishment. "Don't you see what this means?" he cries. "These half-crowns are all bad, and that awful man must have made them on those machines. We must hurry back to the village and let the people know." Only waiting to fill their pockets with the bad coins, they start to dash through the wood.

Rupert finds the old shopman still discussing the trouble with the policeman. Running up to them, the little bear holds up a handful of the shining coins. "What, you again!" roars the shopman. "Didn't I tell you to be off and never come back here?" "Well, I have come back," says Rupert happily. "Do please look at what I've brought you. I've found out all about the bad half-crowns and the man who makes them. You must be quick if you want to catch him."

RUPERT SHOWS THE WAY

The Policeman finds a paving-stone,
And on it specimen coins are thrown.

Their ring is false: "This wicked deed,"
The policeman says, "We'll stop with speed."

The policeman sees the shameful hoard,
And says, "You'll get a grand reward,"

And when he's heard all Rupert's tale,
He says that he the man will trail.

At first the policeman and the shopman are too surprised to know what to do. Then the policeman takes the half-crowns and drops them one by one on a paving-stone. "They're certainly all bad," he says. "We can only follow what he says." Under Rupert's directions he sets off, and soon the strange house comes in view, while the shopman, in great excitement, insists on coming, too.

To their relief the man has not returned, so Rupert leads the policeman into the house and shows him the machines and the mass of half-crowns. "My word, there'll be a fine reward for you," cries the policeman. Then Rupert tells the whole story of how he and Algy came to be there. "We don't want any reward," he says; "we only want our boat and our stores so that we can get on to the seaside."

RUPERT FINDS THE BOAT

Their boat they need, and Algy sees
Upon a nail a bunch of keys.

One works the lock and all their things
They see, when back the shed door swings.

Their boat the shopman helps to lift,
Then goes to fetch the chums a gift.

They wave good-bye, and here you see
They're off again to find the sea.

The old shopman offers to go with Rupert and Algy to try to force open the shed. On their way out there is a shout from Algy: "Look, here's a bunch of keys hanging up. Let's try them." They run to the shed, and to their joy the padlock yields at once. Dragging open the doors they find the precious **boat** inside, as well as their tent and haversacks and **all** their gear.

With much tugging and pushing the two get the boat to the river and launch it, and put all the stuff aboard. Then Rupert turns to thank the old shopman for his help. "Don't thank me," says the old man, "you've done us all a good turn, and if you'll wait I'll bring you a present." He sets off for the village, and in a little while returns with two carriers full of provisions, enough to last them both for **a long voyage.**

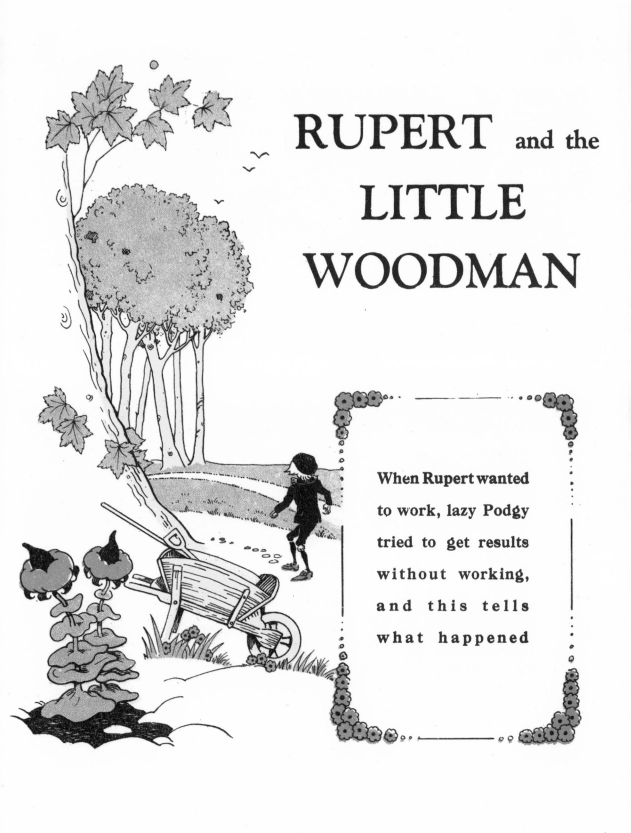

RUPERT and the
LITTLE
WOODMAN

When Rupert wanted
to work, lazy Podgy
tried to get results
without working,
and this tells
what happened

RUPERT HEARS OF WORK

"There's Edward and the Rabbit twins,"
Cries Rupert, and with pleasure grins.

But when he calls, "Do come and play,"
"We can't, we're working hard," they say.

So with them to a hut he walks,
And, seeing them get spades and forks,

He says that he'll go home and hear
If father's got some land this year.

"Hullo, that looks like Edward Trunk and the Rabbit twins," says Rupert, as he peeps through a fence. "I'll see if they'd like to come and play." Hurrying to catch them up, he greets them cheerily, but to his surprise they won't stop. "No play to-day," says Edward importantly, "we're off to do some work; if you like to come with us you shall see what it is." At length Edward and Rex and Reggie reach a wooden hut, and while Rupert waits outside they enter and come out with a wheelbarrow and spades and forks. "Are you going gardening?" asks the little bear. "Not exactly," says Edward in a busy sort of voice. "Our daddies have allotments, and they say we must grow a lot more food this year, so we're going to help." "Ooh," says Rupert, "I wonder if my daddy has an allotment, too."

RUPERT STARTS HIS PLOT

Says Mr. Bear, "A garden plot
I'll give you—you must work a lot!"

"Hurrah!" shouts Rupert, "now I'll show
The boys what lots of food I'll grow."

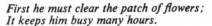

First he must clear the patch of flowers;
It keeps him busy many hours.

And for a bonfire he prepares
While Podgy, all unnoticed, stares.

After a while Mr. Bear comes home, and Rupert immediately jumps up. "Have you an allotment, daddy?" asks the little bear. Mr. Bear looks at him curiously, then he says thoughtfully, "No, but I tell you what—if you like I'll give you one for yourself right in our own garden, and you can clear it and grow food there, only it will mean real work." "Oh, I don't mind work," cries Rupert, as he runs for his gardening tools and follows his father. To Rupert's surprise Mr. Bear gives him a piece of the flower garden as his plot. "You see, we must have less flowers and more food next year," says Mr. Bear, "so you must clear that plot." It is a big plot, and Rupert is soon hard at work. He finds lots of twigs for a bonfire and gets so busy that he doesn't notice his pal Podgy peeping over the fence.

RUPERT BREAKS A BRANCH

He's curious, so he comes to ask
Why Rupert's given himself this task.

"You want a bonfire? Come with me!
My way's as easy as can be."

He finds a tree and grasps a bough;
"See! This will make a bonfire now."

The bough gives way and as they fall
They hear an angry farmer call.

Podgy comes round to ask Rupert what he is doing. "You're just in time to help me work my allotment," says the little bear as he explains his bonfire. "H'm, I don't like work," says Podgy. "There's a tree over there with lots of dead branches. We shall get enough for a huge bonfire in one journey instead of bending our backs picking up hundreds of twigs." Rupert doesn't know if they ought to do it, but Podgy gallops away, so he follows. "Don't bother with that little thing," cries Podgy, "help me with this big branch. It will be enough for a bonfire by itself by the time we've broken it up." Rupert lends his weight, but the branch is more rotten than they think and snaps immediately, tumbling them over. To make matters worse, the angry figure of the farmer appears.

RUPERT FORGIVES PODGY

"What's this? You come and spoil my tree?
Get out, or you will sorry be."

They set off, feeling rather sick,
For Mr. Farmer's got a stick.

Then Podgy says, "I do declare
That after this I'll do my share."

At first he does some strenuous work,
But soon he's tired and wants to shirk.

Rupert and Podgy struggle under the heavy branch, but before they can get clear the farmer is in front of them. "What are you doing on my land," he roars, "and breaking my trees, too? Be off with you before I set about you with my stick." Feeling very shaken, the two pals hurry away. "Oh, dear, I'm so sorry," gasps Podgy; "it's all my fault, because I was too lazy to help with the work you were doing."

Back at home, Podgy turns to Rupert. "I'd like to help you now if you'll let me—just to make amends for getting you into that row with the farmer." "Right ho," cries Rupert, "then we shall make real progress." So they light the bonfire and begin collecting the old greenstuff together. Podgy puffs and pants as he works. "Oh, my," he sighs, "I do wish we could grow things without so much work."

He says, "I can't keep up this pace,"
And sadly mops his sweating face.

He goes to take a shady seat,
Then, squealing, leaps up to his feet.

On Horace Hedgehog he'd sat down,
And Horace runs out with a frown.

He scolds them: "I was fast asleep—
Still in my winter slumber deep."

After a time, poor Podgy gets very hot and tired. "It's no good," he puffs. "I just don't like work! I must sit by this hedge to get my breath back." "Right you are," says Rupert, cheerfully. "I'll carry on by myself until you're better." Scarcely has he moved away when there is a loud squeal. "Ow," cries Podgy, "I sat on something fearfully prickly—whatever can it be?"

While the two pals stand and watch, there is a commotion among the leaves where Podgy was trying to sit down, and a muffled voice comes to them. Then a grumpy little face appears. "Why, it's Horace Hedgehog," cries Rupert. "Yes, and what about it?" grumbles Horace. "Here I've just gone to bed for the winter and some great, heavy creature sits on me and spoils my beauty sleep!"

RUPERT GOES AN ERRAND

And then he adds, "I recommend
The Woodman to my lazy friend."

Towards the wood they're setting out
When Rupert's mother gives a shout;

She sends him to the village shop;
He meets some friends, but cannot stop.

"This Woodman, please, what's his address?"
Asks Rupert. Mr. Chimp can't guess.

Podgy explains why he had to sit down. "So you don't like work," chuckles Horace. "The only man who knows how to grow things without work is the Little Woodman; you'd better ask him." "Who is the Little Woodman?" asks Rupert. "Let's go into the wood and see if we can find him." But as they are starting there is a call from the cottage. It is Mrs. Bear, who wants Rupert to run an errand.

Rupert takes the basket and makes for the village, passing Lily Duckling and Willie Whiskers, who are hurrying home across the common. "You'd better buck up," says Lily, "there's an awful storm coming." In the village shop Rupert asks, but can get no news of the Little Woodman. "There are lots of woodmen in the forest," says Mr. Chimp, "but they are all big, strong people."

RUPERT HEARS A VOICE

He hurries home to miss the rain
And hears a voice he can't explain.

He thinks it's coming from a tree,
Now who, he wonders, can it be?

A branch that's fallen blocks a crack,
So Rupert strives to push it back.

A tiny man he sees appear,
Who says, "You know, I'm master here."

Rupert runs before the storm, doing his best to get home without getting wet. As he is passing the trees a strange sound comes to his ears. The sound seems to be coming from inside a huge crack in the tree, and a great branch has blown down and is blocking up the entrance. "Help!" cries the voice, "I can't get out." "Cheer up," shouts Rupert. "I'll see what I can do."

At the end of the great bough Rupert finds a shorter branch, and by using that as a lever he manages to heave the whole thing away from the tree. A little door flies open and a tiny man pops out and beams at him. "I'm sure I'm very much obliged to you," he grins. "B-but who are you?" gasps Rupert. "Why, don't you know?" answers the other. "I'm in charge of this wood and all that grows in it."

RUPERT TO THE RESCUE

"And if inside the tree you'll pop
You'll see my little woodland shop.

"Just now I'm working many nours
In mixing colours for the flowers."

"My friend," says Rupert, "wants to know
If things, without hard work, will grow."

"This ice-cream plant requires no toil;
It grows at once in any soil."

"Why, you must be the little woodman whom Horace Hedgehog spoke of," exclaims Rupert. Suddenly the rain starts falling. "Come and shelter," shouts the other, seizing the little bear's basket. Pushing in head first, Rupert can just squeeze through the tiny entrance, and finds himself in a queer sort of workshop right in the heart of the tree. "There," says the little man, "this is where I control everything in the wood. "Please," says the little bear rather shyly, "my friend Podgy wants to find a vegetable that will grow without working and without waiting. Could you help us?" The woodman looks thoughtful, and then he fetches a bottle. "These are seeds of a very rare ice-cream plant," he says. "It grows in a day and in any weather and in any soil."

RUPERT IN THE SNOW

Then Rupert sees it's getting late,
And says he must no longer wait.

He's given two seeds, and turns to go,
But finds the ground all white with snow.

When Rupert's errand has been done,
To talk to Podgy he must run.

"Why," Podgy says, "these seeds are grand!
Let's plant them here, just where we stand."

The little woodman gives Rupert two of the valuable seeds, which the little bear puts carefully into his pocket. Then he glances at a clock. "Good gracious," he gasps, "my mother will think I'm lost. I must run." Struggling up through the tiny doorway, he finds to his surprise that the rain has turned to a heavy snowstorm and the ground is covered in white. The little man shows him the shortest way home, and off he trots. After taking his shopping-basket home Rupert goes out again. "Any luck?" shouts Podgy. "Rather!" cries Rupert. "I found the little woodman." He explains all about the new vegetable that needs neither work nor waiting. "That suits me splendidly," says Podgy. In great excitement they then scrape the snow from a patch of bare earth and just drop the seeds in.

RUPERT PLANTS THE SEEDS

But Mr. Bear thinks he will read
About this easy-growing seed.

The seed's not known, and Mr. Bear
Says, "Of all easy things, beware!"

Next morning Rupert Bear looks out,
And gives a most excited shout;

The plants have grown up strong and tall,
And Podgy Pig has come to call.

Rupert is very full of his adventure, and when he gets home he tells his father all about the little woodman and points to where he has planted the seeds. Mr. Bear is quite mystified. He searches through all his gardening books, but can discover nothing about the new vegetable. "It's a strange plant if it gives good results without your doing any work," he says thoughtfully. "Nothing good comes without work. I advise you to be careful." Next morning Rupert jumps out of bed, and the first things he thinks about are the new vegetables. To his amazement they are already half grown. He dashes out in the snow to examine them just as Podgy pops his head over the fence and Mrs. Bear peeps out to see what the excitement is about. "Come on in and look at them," shouts Rupert to Podgy.

RUPERT PULLS THE CROP

"Look," Podgy says, his face abeam,
"The fruit looks just like rich ice cream."

Now Rupert to Mamma gives one,
But Podgy gobbles his for fun.

"The woodman we must see again,"
Cried Podgy, "and more seeds obtain."

But half-way there he feels so ill,
He groans and has to stand quite still.

Rupert returns quickly, and to his astonishment the weird plants have grown still more, and on each one is a curious fruit something like an ice-cream. Eagerly they pick them and Podgy at once takes a bite, while Rupert unselfishly gives his to Mrs. Bear. "What a curious looking thing," says she, doubtfully. "It's perfectly scrumptious," cries Podgy, licking his lips; "it's just like a real ice-cream, and oh, my, isn't it cold!" When the new ice-fruit is finished, Podgy smiles happily. "That was lovely," he cries. "Come along! We must find that little woodman and get lots more of those seeds." Rupert starts to run with him, but before they are half-way to the wood Podgy suddenly stops and leans against a fence. "Golly, I do feel funny," he says; "I've never felt like this before."

RUPERT IS WORRIED

"I'm going home," he says, "I fear
It's that new fruit that's made me queer."

Then Rupert finds Mamma feels sick,
And says he'll fetch the Doctor quick.

He runs across the snow, pell-mell;
"Please Doctor, come, Mamma's not well."

The Doctor of his tale takes note,
Then says he'll fetch his hat and coat.

Podgy gets no better, and all at once he makes up his mind to hurry home to bed. He dashes away, and Rupert is just about to follow when an awful thought strikes him. He had given his own ice-fruit to his mother. What if it had made her feel ill, too? In great anxiety he turns and runs into his home. Sure enough, Mrs. Bear is in an armchair, looking very weak and unhappy. "It was the new fruit!" gasps Rupert. "And it's my fault. What shall I do?" Rupert loses no time in running for Dr. Lion, and he is lucky in finding the clever old doctor at home. "Please, can you come quickly?" pleads the little bear. "My mummy has eaten an ice-cream plant and it has made her feel awfully queer." "Bless my soul," says the doctor, "but what is an ice-cream plant?"

RUPERT GETS THE DOCTOR

They find poor Mrs. Bear in bed,
And Dr. Lion shakes his head:

"Her temperature," he says, "is low,
But how to treat her I don't know."

"The woodman," Rupert says, "I'll tell;
Perhaps an antidote he'll sell."

He finds the tracks he made before,
And soon he's knocking at the door.

Dr. Lion can make nothing of Mrs. Bear's case. "It's a very strange illness indeed," he says. "By this thermometer her temperature is right down—lower than anything I have seen. Show me one of your wonderful ice-cream plants." But, of course, Rupert has to explain that both of them are eaten, and, after much worrying, the poor old doctor admits that he is baffled by the whole affair. "It's very serious," he says, "but I just don't know what to do." Rupert decides to tell the little woodman all about it. In the forest he loses his way and asks a wandering fox to guide him, but the sly animal will give him no help at all. Suddenly Rupert pauses and gazes at the ground. "These footprints," he murmurs, "why, they must be my own footprints of yesterday, and if I follow them back they must lead me to the right tree."

Rupert and the Little Woodman

RUPERT TELLS THE WOODMAN

The woodman says, in great distress,
"To cure fat Podgy's laziness

"I sent those seeds, but look, my dear,
At these big sunny seeds I've here.

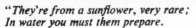

"They're from a sunflower, very rare;
In water you must them prepare.

"They'll melt the cream without delay,
And mother's pain will go away."

The little woodman looks very serious when he hears Rupert's story. "My plans have gone wrong," he says. "You said that your friend Podgy wanted the seeds because he didn't like work, and I meant them to be for him only. The vegetable is terribly indigestible, and I wanted to teach him a lesson." Then, leading the way underground, he seizes a large bottle full of big seeds which glow with light. "Those

look lovely," says Rupert. "Whatever are they?" Picking up a pair of tongs, the little woodman carefully lifts out a few of the glowing seeds, puts them into a smaller bottle, and gives them to Rupert. "You see," says the little man, "the fruit of that ice-plant I gave you tastes very nice, but it's very cold and takes about a week to melt after you've swallowed it, so it's no wonder your poor mother's temperature is down."

RUPERT BRINGS THE CURE

While Rupert runs fast as he can,
He's followed by the tiny man;

He mixes well the sunshine pill,
And Mrs. Bear soon feels less ill.

As Rupert gratefully sets out
To thank the man, he hears a shout.

And sees the woodman, whose desire
Is after Podgy's health to enquire.

Thanking the little woodman for his kindness, Rupert struggles up from the tiny doorway and goes full pelt homewards without looking back, and not noticing that the little man is quietly following him. Mrs. Bear is looking more pale and ill than ever. Quickly Rupert takes one of the glowing sunflower seeds and makes her swallow it with some water. "There, that's better," sighs Rupert, as more life comes into her face. "My word! I'll never meddle with those unknown vegetables again."

When his mother is better Rupert goes out again. He is startled to hear his name called, and there is the little man peeping at him round a corner. "I'm interested in this business," said the woodman. "I've an idea that your friend Podgy must be feeling sorry for himself, too. I want to go to him."

RUPERT STARTS WORK AGAIN

When Mrs. Pig admits the pair
Poor Podgy's nearly in despair.

"You shirked your work," the woodman cries;
"Now let this illness make you wise."

Soon Podgy's up and freely owns
His error, in most humble tones.

And Rupert's Father says, "We'll grow,
In future, just the things we know."

The two companions are quickly admitted by Podgy's mother, and they find poor Podgy groaning and looking very blue. To Rupert's amazement the little woodman doesn't show any sympathy, but kicks off his shoes and jumps on the bed. "I hope you've learnt your lesson by now," he says sternly. "If I cure you, you must promise never to be so lazy again." Podgy promises, and Rupert produces the sunflower seeds. Rupert and the little woodman return the next day and find that Podgy is quite himself again.

"You've taught me a lesson," he says as he seizes their hands. "I know now that no good results can come without work." Then the little woodman hurries back to his duties in the wood, and Rupert is soon helping his daddy once more.

RUPERT and the

SUGAR BIRD

"A story of how
a kind action by
Rupert to a little
bird saves him
from trouble"

Rupert and the Sugar Bird

RUPERT MEETS A STRANGER

While Rupert reads a story book,
His mother cries, "Come here and look,"

A pink-white bird has perched nearby;
To see it closer he will try.

It's quickly out of sight again,
And Rupert's chase has been in vain.

He sees the brothers Fox, but they
Turn round and run the other way.

One day Rupert has nothing to do, so he takes a book and begins to read. He has not read far when he is interrupted by Mrs. Bear. "Come and look here, Rupert," she says in a strange voice.

He quickly joins her at the window, and, gazing out, he sees a plump pink-and-white bird sitting on a branch. "What an odd-looking creature," says the little bear. "It might almost be made of sugar."

Hurriedly putting on his scarf Rupert goes out, only to find that the queer bird has disappeared.

"It's no good," he sighs, "nobody can run as fast as a bird flying; I'd better go home again."

On regaining the lane he sees the two brothers, Freddy and Ferdy Fox, ahead of him.

To his surprise, the Foxes turn and run the other way.

RUPERT IS PUZZLED

The Foxes have quite disappeared;
Says Rupert, "Everything's most weird."

Then birds he sees, all chattering round
An object lying on the ground.

He hurries quickly to the spot:
A sugar Easter egg they've got.

"Who can have brought it?" croaks a crow,
"That's what we birds all want to know."

On reaching the place where the Foxes were, Rupert finds that they, too, have disappeared. Further on he pauses by a fence and peeps through. A lot of sparrows and thrushes and crows are hovering round a certain spot in the field and are chattering loudly. "There must be something interesting in the grass," thinks the little bear. "I'd like to go and see what it is. Surely they wouldn't fly away from me too."

Climbing the fence, Rupert reaches the place where the birds are settling round a smooth round object in the grass. He picks it up and finds it very heavy. "Why, it's a huge Easter Egg," he gasps, "and made of sugar. What on earth is it doing here?" "That's just what we'd like to know," croaks an old crow, "the real question is—who brought it? It's a very serious matter."

RUPERT SHOWS THE EGG

The sugar bird again appears,
Flies up to Rupert, "Thief!" he jeers;

His mother says, "It puzzles me;
Ask Mrs. Sheep what it can be."

Says Mrs. Sheep, "No eggs are here,
It's early for them yet, my dear."

Then Rupert sees the Wise Old Goat
Who on a problem new will dote.

Rupert is impressed by what the crow has said and runs home to ask his mother. On the way the queer bird he had been chasing suddenly appears and flies straight for him. "Thief! Thief! Thief!" screeches the bird. At home, Mrs. Bear also is very puzzled by the egg. "It may have been taken from the sweet shop," she suggests. "I should trot along and ask old Mrs. Sheep if she has missed it."

Hastening to the sweet shop Rupert shows the egg. Mrs. Sheep looks at him in astonishment. "It hasn't been stolen from here," she says.

Rupert, more mystified than ever, starts home-wards. While crossing a field he sees the familiar figure of the Wise Old Goat. "He's just the man. He loves solving mysteries," thinks the little bear. "I'll ask him."

RUPERT GETS ADVICE

The Goat hears Rupert's tale all through,
Then says, "Here's my advice to you:

Replace the egg upon the ground
Exactly where it first was found."

He hasn't gone so very far,
When angry birds cry, "There you are."

One takes the egg, and others say,
"Explain! How came that egg your way."

The Wise Old Goat is very surprised at seeing the egg and listens carefully to what Rupert tells him. "There's something suspicious about this," he says gravely. "Nobody ought to have Easter eggs as early as this. My advice to you is—put it back exactly where you found it."

Rupert thanks him and moves rather sadly away. "It seems a pity," he thinks, "it's such a lovely egg."

Rupert has no chance of carrying out his intention. At the sound of heavy wings he turns and finds several large birds swooping towards him. One of them seizes the egg from his hands and flies off with it. "Why, I believe you are all made of sugar!" he gasps. "Never mind that," says a bird sternly. "The point is: a lot of eggs have been stolen and we find you holding one of them. How do you explain that?"

Rupert and the Sugar Bird

RUPERT SHOWS THE WAY

"We don't believe you," cries a bird;
"Show us the field where this occurred."

They reach the spot, up flies a crow,
Who says, "He's not a thief, I know."

"Someone's a thief," the birds declare;
"We mean to hunt him everywhere."

Then Rupert finds, exhausted, weak,
The bird he'd earlier gone to seek.

Rupert insists that he did not steal the egg. "I found it in a field," he exclaims. "A likely tale!" sneers the great bird. "Show us which field you mean."

They obviously do not believe him. Luckily for the little bear a crow has seen what has happened, and in a few moments the sparrows and thrushes have crowded round. "Rupert didn't steal the egg," they cry, "it was here before he came to take it away."

At length the sugar birds believe that Rupert is telling the truth.

After thanking the crows for their help, Rupert starts for home. To his surprise he sees the original sugar bird sitting on a post, and looking very exhausted. "Oh dear," it groans. "I'm all in, I've flown around for days searching for thieves, and I can't go on."

RUPERT GIVES A LIFT

Says Rupert, "If the way you'll show,
I'll take you where you want to go."

About the eggs he asks in vain;
The rested bird flies off again.

Then in the distance Rupert spies,
The Brothers Fox; "Hey! Wait!" he cries,

And then, "Dear me! They've run away;
That's twice they've played that trick to-day."

"You poor thing," says Rupert kindly. "Do let me help you." "I must get home," gasps the sugar bird. "Then you must let me carry you part of the way," insists the little bear. Guided by the bird he finds himself in strange country.

At length they reach some high cliffs, and the sugar bird, now refreshed, leaves his arms and soars over the top.

Rupert ponders over the mystery without making anything of it. Just as he is giving it up he spies two little figures emerging from some trees down below. With excitement he recognises the Fox brothers. Perhaps they can explain things. "Hi!" he shouts, as he runs down the hill. To his amazement, when he reaches the spot the foxes have disappeared.

Rupert and the Sugar Bird

RUPERT LOSES HIS WAY

Thinks Rupert, *"This is country queer;*
Why did that bird direct me here?"

Then looking down he gets a shock;
A tunnel leads right through the rock.

The tunnel has such narrow walls,
On hands and knees he bravely crawls;

And when he comes out in the light,
He sees a fence of monstrous height.

Failing to see anything of the foxes, Rupert determines to explore the strange wood. It is full of great boulders, and is absolutely silent and deserted. With a shock he sees that a tunnel opens right at his feet and goes sloping down into the very heart of the rock. It looks very gloomy, and for a while he hesitates. Then, screwing up his courage, he steps gingerly down into the darkness.

The tunnel is very narrow and irregular, so that Rupert has to go on his hands and knees. At length he reaches the bottom, and as he starts on the upward slope the light meets him and he emerges on the other side of the cliff barrier. Before him is a huge wooden fence, which hides all the view. "My word! There must be something important behind that for anyone to build such a strong fence."

RUPERT MEETS A SOLDIER

To find an entrance he decides,
And round the fencing boldly strides;

A chocolate soldier cries, "Beware!
All Easter eggs are in my care."

The sentry shouts, the gates fly wide,
And soldiers run from every side.

Before the sugar judge he's brought,
Who says, "So, after all, you're caught."

Rupert thinks of trying to scramble up the fence, but the barbed wire on top makes him give up that idea. Running round the supports, he soon reaches a little chocolate soldier in a sentry-box, who has been gazing at him speechlessly, but who gets his voice back. "This is the home of the sugar birds and the chocolate birds," he says. "All the Easter eggs in the world come from here. But who are you? And what are you doing here?"

When he has recovered from his surprise at seeing Rupert, the sentry gives a loud shout. Instantly the gates fly open, little chocolate soldiers and sugar soldiers come running up, and the little bear finds himself hustled in front of a sugar magistrate. One of the large sugar birds is there and eyes Rupert curiously. "So they caught you after all," he says. "I thought your story was a bit weak!"

RUPERT IS CAPTURED

"Of Easter eggs we've been bereft;
We think you're guilty of the theft."

Then on the way to jail the bird
That Rupert helped, cries, "What's occurred?"

They find the sugar judge again,
And Rupert's honesty explain.

Then says the judge, "The tunnel show;
A soldier true with you shall go."

Rupert explains just how he got there, but the magistrate isn't satisfied. "There has been a serious theft of eggs," he says sternly, "and you're the only person we've caught so far. You will be locked up until we can find if you're speaking the truth."

Suddenly there is a flutter of wings. "Why, it is Rupert!" cries a voice: "what are they doing to you?"

"This will never do," says the Sugar Bird. At a word from him the little soldiers march Rupert back to the sugar magistrate and the bird confirms the truth of everything that Rupert had said. "In that case," says the magistrate, "there is nothing to do but to let you go; but I do wish you would show us how you got here. We must have that tunnel blocked up." Rupert agrees.

RUPERT IS RELEASED

He shows the tunnel, black as coal;
"Don't think," he says, "it's just a hole,

"But won't you let me stay with you?
I'd like to help you find a clue."

"Well," says the soldier, "come with me;
First see our specially guarded tree.

"And now this ladder climb," he cries;
"Up there you'll get a big surprise."

Rupert points out the entrance to the tunnel. "Good gracious," says the soldier, "can one get through there?" Rupert prepares to leave for home. Then an idea strikes him and he turns suddenly. "It seems silly," he says, "to go back with the mystery still unsolved. Won't you let me stay and help you?" "Why, that's topping of you," says the chocolate soldier as he shakes his hand warmly.

"If you're going to help us you had better learn something about what goes on here," says the chocolate soldier, as he hurries Rupert through the main building. At the back a great tree comes into view. The soldier, however, finds a secret path through the spikes and hoists a ladder against the trunk. "Up you go, Rupert," he says; "there's a surprise waiting for you up there."

RUPERT SEES THE NEST

The tree is simply crammed with nests;
A sugar bird in each one rests.

A tree for chocolate birds is near,
For Easter eggs are all laid here.

"Well," says the bird upon the ground,
"Have you an explanation found?"

They haven't yet, and so explore
The sentry-guarded, locked-up store.

Half-way up the tree Rupert pauses and looks around in astonishment. The great tree is crammed with nests, and on each nest sits a sugar bird. "You see," says the little soldier, "this is where all the sugar Easter eggs come from." In the distance is another huge tree. "That," says the little man, "is where the chocolate birds live. All the chocolate eggs in the world come from there."

Descending the tree Rupert finds a gloomy-looking sugar bird waiting for him. "Well," says the bird, "I suppose the little bear hasn't found any clue?" "Not yet," says Rupert cheerfully. "I want to see where the eggs were stolen from." So the chocolate soldier takes him to the great store-rooms. "There," he says, "all the eggs are kept behind those strong doors until they're wanted for Easter."

RUPERT GETS AN IDEA

The finest eggs from every nest
Are padlocked in an iron chest.

The soldier says: "A shocking theft!"
And Rupert: "Let's spread out what's left."

Inside the chest they find a hole;
Says Rupert, "Look, through there they stole."

So off they run the fence to inspect;
That's where they'll find the great defect.

"This chest," says the soldier, "has the very finest eggs. Nobody seems to have been here—the padlocks haven't been disturbed, and yet when the chest was inspected last week half the eggs had gone!" "My word!" says Rupert, "that really is a mystery." He sits down thoroughly puzzled. Suddenly he jumps up. "I've got an idea," he cries, "let's take out all the eggs that are left."

When most of the eggs are out, Rupert points in excitement. "Just as I thought," he shouts, "the lid wasn't opened, so the eggs must have gone through the bottom—look, there's the hole that the thieves must have made!" "Why," gasps the chocolate soldier, "to do that they must have found a hole in the barricade just behind this great chest." Now they are hot on the trail and the pair run out again.

RUPERT SOLVES THE PUZZLE

Cries Rupert, "See! the fault is here."
And thinks "The Foxes have been queer."

Back through the tunnelled rock he crawls;
"Hallo!" the bird he rescued calls.

They tell their story to a crow,
Who says, "I'll show you where to go."

Inside a hut the Foxes groan;
"We ate the eggs, we're ill," they moan.

At length Rupert stops. "There you are," he
cries. "That board has rotted away. The thieves
must have wriggled through there and right into the
back of that chest." While the chocolate soldier
dashes back to spread the news, Rupert runs into the
tunnel through which he had come. His thoughts
fly back to the queer behaviour of the two foxes.
"They must be the culprits," he mutters.

As Rupert hurries away from the tunnel he meets
an old crow. He explains his haste, and the crow
immediately makes him turn aside and leads him to
another part of the wood where a round hut is
hidden away. "The foxes have been using that hut
for days," he says. Sure enough, Rupert finds what
he had expected. Two sacks of lovely eggs are there
and on the floor sits Freddy and Ferdy Fox.

RUPERT GETS A SURPRISE

"We've saved two sacksfull," Rupert cries;
The sugar bird for helpers flies.

Then for the Foxes Rupert begs,
"Don't punish them, they're sick of eggs."

The Foxes see the birds take wing,
Then gradually to their rescuer cling.

And Rupert's sent, on Easter Day,
The finest egg the birds could lay.

When the sugar bird sees Rupert dragging out the sacks of precious eggs it flies swiftly away, returning in a few minutes with the powerful sugar birds. "So," cries the biggest bird, "you have found the thieves. We will carry them to the sugar magistrate for punishment." "Oh, no! Please leave them alone," pleads Rupert, "they've already suffered enough and are feeling so ill. Won't you let them go?"

The sugar birds are surprised at Rupert's request, but since he has solved the mystery they agree to let the foxes go. "Oh, Rupert," says Ferdy, "what idiots we have been. But for you we might be having a dreadful time now. On Easter Day a large parcel arrives for Rupert, and in it he finds the finest sugar egg he has ever seen—a present from the sugar birds as reward for solving their mystery.